Dark Harbor Haunting

Clarissa Ross

Dark Harbor Haunting

Dark Harbor
#4

Five Star
Unity, Maine

Five Star Romance Series.

Published in 2001 in conjunction with the
Maureen Moran Agency.

Set in 11 pt. Plantin by Al Chase.

Printed in the United States on permanent paper.

Library of Congress Cataloging-in-Publication Data

Ross, Clarissa, 1912–
    Dark Harbor haunting / Clarissa Ross.
      p.   cm. — (Dark Harbor series ; bk. 4)
    ISBN 0-7862-2937-3 (hc : alk. paper)
    1. Gothic fiction. gsafd   I. Title.
PR9199.3.R5996 D28 2001
   813′.54—dc21   00-062267

To Beryl and Gordon Spencer
and the fun nights in the
music room!

CHAPTER ONE

Jean Rivers, a feature writer for the *Boston Globe*, wrote many interesting New England fact articles, concentrating on the occult and some of the eerie hauntings so common in that area. Perhaps the most exciting of these assignments had been her visit to Dark Harbor, an ancient fishing and tourist center on Pirate Island, some thirty miles out in the ocean from Cape Cod.

Captain Zachary Miller in Dark Harbor told her the weird tale of a young woman who had come there in 1895 to avenge her own murder . . .

When she'd first heard the story, Jean thought it the most incredible yarn which had ever come her way. When she'd written an account of what the old Captain told her and published it in the weekly edition of the *Globe*, the majority of her readers agreed it was a fascinating and extraordinary tale.

Her going to Pirate Island had come about in an almost casual way. Her city editor, Jeff Goodwin, had called her into his office one day in early September and suggested the trip.

Leaning back in his swivel chair the blond, youngish Jeff had smiled as he said, "How would you like to leave the mainland for a while?"

She'd stared at him in surprise. "What have you in mind now? Don't tell me there's a Beauty Contest or a Dog Show in Bermuda you want me to cover!" She was a pert, raven-haired girl in her twenties who'd graduated from Boston

University to her job on the paper. While she was not a beauty she had a neat, well-scrubbed look and an even-featured, intelligent face.

"Not nearly as far as Bermuda," Jeff said. "Ever hear of Dark Harbor?"

"Of course," she replied at once. "That's the chief town on Pirate Island. The island is reached by ferry from Cape Cod."

"Right," Jeff agreed. "And there is limited air service from the mainland as well."

She frowned slightly. "Isn't that where there was a hippie colony camped in a monastery? A monastery which had once been a hospital for lepers?"

"You have a good memory," Jeff smiled. "There was a big drug scandal tied in with the hippie colony and it was broken up. A lot of intriguing stories have come out of Pirate Island."

She gave him a knowing glance. "And now you think I might come up with another one?"

"Correct."

"I guessed that," she said with mock dismay. Jeff was one of her favorite people. "Go on."

He leaned forward with his arms on the desk as he told her, "I have a good friend living there. Interesting chap by the name of Derek Mills."

"I always worry a little about your interesting friends," Jean told the young editor wryly. "The last one you introduced me to turned out to be a secret agent and I nearly found myself jailed for associating with him."

"That was an unfortunate mistake on my part," the young man apologized.

"They always are," she told him. "Go on!"

"Derek Mills is a most reliable person, he is Director of the Dark Harbor Museum. His family is one of the oldest on the island and wealthy. Derek gives a great deal of his time to local causes."

"Sounds dedicated."

"You'll like him," Jeff promised.

"I hope better than that secret agent," she grimaced.

"This is altogether different," the editor assured her. "In his position Derek has his fingers on the pulse of the island. I'm positive he'll be able to put you on to something good."

"You really think so?"

"I do. If you haven't visited the island you'll find it an unusual spot. At worst you can settle for a travel article about it and at best you can perhaps dig up another one of those spooky, haunted house items."

"I've done enough of them!" she scoffed.

"People are always interested in them, I promise you," he said. "At this time of year the tourist traffic on Cape Cod and the island will be slow and it will be a pleasant time for a visit."

She sat back with a sigh. "I can tell you're determined I'll go."

"I'd like you to," he agreed. "I'm sure you and Derek will hit it off."

Jean gave him a teasing glance. "Are you matchmaking again? Because you know I ended my engagement, you keep trying to dig up interesting men for me. The trouble is most of them are weird."

"Derek is married," Jeff said.

"So that settles that," Jean replied. "And I'm glad. I like to keep strictly to business on these excursions."

Jeff looked mildly reproachful. "You don't appreciate my efforts to find you the ideal husband?"

"No."

"Too bad," the young editor said. "I mean so well."

"I know you do."

"About this Derek Mills," he went on. "He is married but his wife is away at present."

"Oh?"

"I don't mean there's trouble between them," he went on hastily. "It's just that she hasn't been well for some years. She has spent most of her time in a mental hospital here on the mainland."

"That's too bad," Jean said sympathetically.

"It is a tragedy for Derek. The last I heard she may not recover and yet she lives on. It has cast a shadow over his life."

"There are no children?"

"No. There was a child and she was killed in a fall from the island cliffs. That marked the start of his wife's descent into insanity."

"It surely is a tragic story."

"So that's the background of Derek Mills. I see him every so often when he comes to Boston on business for the museum. He's confided that he has met several interesting girls, but as long as his wife lives I'm certain he is likely to remain faithful to her."

Jean said, "You make him sound more pleasant than any of your other friends I've met."

"Good," Jeff said. "Now my idea is to have Derek introduce you to the island. He'll know all the characters and where you may locate the best stories. I've booked a room at a motel in Dark Harbor and you can take your car over with you. You'll find Derek in his office at the museum."

"When do you want me to leave?" she asked.

"I've spoken to Derek on the phone," Jeff said. "I told him you'll be driving down to the Cape tomorrow and taking the boat over. He's invited you to have dinner with him on your first night on the island."

She stared at him in disbelief. "You made all those arrangements without even consulting me?"

Jeff chuckled. "I was sure you'd go."

Jean got to her feet. "That's what's wrong with our relationship. You're much too sure of me! I suppose since you've taken care of everything I'll have to go."

The young editor was on his feet. "Derek Mills is looking forward to meeting you."

"Fine," she said dryly.

"He'll call at your motel around seven on the night of your arrival. From there on you can work it out."

She shook her head. "Really? I wonder that you don't have a day to day schedule for my entire stay on the island."

"I'll make one up if you like."

"Never!" she said, raising a hand in protest. "I find my stories in my own way."

"Bring us back a really weird one!" he told her as he saw her to the door of the office.

"I can't promise a thing," she said. "I don't know anything about the island. There may be no good possibilities."

"I can promise you there are," Jeff said. "Get Derek to introduce you to some of the old sea captains. Dark Harbor was once an important whaling port. There are a lot of old-timers still around."

That was how it began. The rest of that day she spent getting herself and her car ready for the trip. She found there was a ferry that took cars leaving early in the afternoon. If she left Boston reasonably early in the morning she could reach Hyannis in time for lunch before the ferry. This would get her to Dark Harbor late in the afternoon.

She also did some background reading on the island. From all accounts Pirate Island had reached its peak of prosperity in the early nineteenth century. During this period ships from the island sailed the seven seas in pursuit of the valuable whale oil. But by 1870 the demand for this oil ended and the island became depressed. Not until the turn of the century did prosperity return to the islanders. Then fishing on a large commercial scale brought fresh activity and money to the area.

And in modern days the quaint island had become a noted tourist resort. Each summer thousands visited the island and there were many who lived there in summer homes. With the approach of autumn the single movie house and most of the restaurants shut down. But a hard core of residents maintained a pleasant life on the small island the year through.

The next morning Jean drove her small red sports car down the four-lane route to the Cape. The summer traffic was over and she was able to enjoy the drive. She wondered about both the island and Derek Mills. From Jeff's description he sounded like an interesting young man. Yet, despite all this, she had a strange feeling of apprehension about going to the island.

After a pleasant luncheon in a motel dining room which overlooked the wharves of Hyannis, she drove her car on the ferry and found herself a place on deck. Again she was fortunate. It was midweek and the rush of tourists was over so the ship had few passengers. As the ferry left the wharf she stood by the railing to study the receding mainland.

A voice at her elbow said, "We're saying goodbye to Cape Cod for a while."

She turned to find herself looking at an elderly, white-haired man with a pleasant face. He was wearing a brown tweed suit and a light trench coat. Something about his lined, tan face suggested the air of a professional man.

She said, "I was just thinking that. Our next view of land will be Pirate Island."

The old man's eyes twinkled. "Have you been to the island before?"

"No."

"I didn't recognize you," he said. "And I know almost everyone on the island. May I introduce myself, my name is Taylor, Dr. Henry Taylor."

"How do you do," she said with a smile. "I'm Jean Rivers and I write feature stories for the *Boston Globe*."

"I've seen your by-line," Dr. Henry Taylor said at once. "You did a series about shipwrecks."

She nodded, pleased that he knew her work. "Among other things," she said.

"And now you're going to do a story about the island?" he suggested.

"I hope to," she said. "If something of interest comes along. I'm meeting the director of the museum, Derek Mills. And I hope through him to get some stories."

"Of course," the old doctor said. "I know Mills well. A fine young man. He'll take pleasure in helping you."

"I'm looking forward to meeting him."

"Have him introduce you to Captain Zachary Miller," the doctor said. "He's a veteran skipper. Once Joseph Conrad sailed with him on a freighter and his father and grandfather were both captains. He's in his eighties now and can tell you more tales about Dark Harbor than anyone else."

"Captain Miller," she said. "I must remember his name."

"Derek is bound to mention him in any case," Dr. Taylor said. "We've been hosts to nearly every kind of people on the island. Over the years we've had Puritans, Satanists, pirates, wreckers, smugglers, whalers, hedonists, ordinary fishing folk and tourists."

She laughed. "At least you can boast variety."

The old doctor nodded and brought a pipe out from his

coat pocket as he stared across the broad expanse of ocean ahead of them. "Out there beyond the horizon she lies. Much of the land is covered by barren shrubs and rocks which cannot be cultivated. The few fertile areas have been developed by farmers or have been taken over by the fine estates scattered outside Dark Harbor. And part way along the island, between Dark Harbor and Gull Light, there is even a section of evergreen forest."

"Dark Harbor is the principal town?"

"Yes. That is where I have my practice and where the museum and all the other public buildings are located."

"You make it sound like an interesting place," she told him as he turned against the wind to light his pipe.

He turned to her again and, puffing on his pipe, said, "I have lived there the best part of my life. I know the people and most of their family histories. The superstitious maintain that those who visit our bleak island far out in the Atlantic are never quite the same again. Maybe some of our thick fogs seep into their brains, but most people, who come to know the island and leave it, are always haunted by it afterward."

The old man's solemn pronouncement struck her with the same chill apprehension she'd experienced earlier. That strange sensation that she was heading towards an unknown danger, something which she didn't fully understand.

She stared at the old doctor. "As a medical man, do you believe in ghosts?"

He took his pipe from his mouth and stared grimly at the water. "I think I'd be a liar if I said I didn't. And perhaps a fool as well. Yes, I think there are such things as ghosts, and ESP and all the rest."

"So you are a mystic as well as a doctor," she suggested.

"In a very modest way."

"Did you take any interest in the Satanist group which

held forth in the old monastery?"

"Only to try and clear the island of them," he said with a touch of anger. "That was a drug ring operating in the guise of a cult. They caused a great deal of trouble on the island. I was glad when the police caught up with them and they were forced to leave."

"Wasn't that monastery a leper colony years ago?"

Dr. Henry Taylor said, "Yes. A ship foundered off the island in the early days, one of many such wrecks, but the crew of this one was riddled with leprosy. They remained to live in several of the fishing villages and soon they passed the disease on to some of the islanders. By the time the doctor who lived here found out what had happened, the disease had made fearful inroads. A religious order volunteered to build the monastery and care for the lepers. It was built and operated for years with government aid until the last of the lepers died. Then the monks sold the monastery and it has been used for many things since."

"That was how the Satanists managed to get it?"

"Yes. Now it has been turned into a tourist hotel and hopefully it will continue to operate as one. By the way, where are you staying?"

"At the Gray Heron," she said.

His eyebrows raised. "That is the only hotel to stay open all through the year. It is well-situated on the main street, but I should warn you it's not our best place."

"Oh?"

"It will do, mind you," he hastened to say. "And it is an ancient building in which you'll get a feel of the island's history. The tavern adjoining it also does a good business. The man who operates the Gray Heron is Matthew Kimble, he's past middle age and a bit dour. Quite a character! There have been plenty of rumors about him."

She was at once interested. "Such as?"

"One of them concerns his grandfather. They claim the old man made a fortune in black ivory."

"Black ivory?" The term was new to her.

The old doctor smiled bleakly. "The slave trade, my dear. You know a number of Yankees were involved in it. Their fast sailing ships made it easy for them to operate."

"And so that was how the Kimble family fortune was founded?"

"Yes, if what I've heard is true. Matthew went to the mainland as a young man. His father and mother were running the hotel then. It is said he committed some serious crime and spent several years in prison. One foggy night he returned to the island much to everyone's surprise. His father had died and his mother was ailing. He took over the operation of the inn and he's been here ever since. Yet don't count on getting any help from him, he's close-mouthed and bitter. Most people are wary around him."

"I'll remember that," she said.

"But you'll find the inn interesting all the same," was Dr. Taylor's prediction. "How long do you expect to remain in Dark Harbor?"

"Long enough to do some stories," she said. "I suppose a week or maybe two at the most."

"Then perhaps I shall see you again," the old doctor suggested. "I have a small, modern hospital annex off my house. It is really an extension of my office. But it enables me to treat patients there as they would be looked after in any small hospital."

"I'll call on you," she said. "There could be a story in that."

"Don't think I'm looking for publicity," he protested.

"I know you aren't," she said. "But I think readers might like to know about your hospital."

16

"You must also visit the Old Mill," Dr. Taylor said. "It's in Dark Harbor and was built in 1746. Once around the turn of the century it was offered for sale as firewood for twenty dollars. But as soon as the Historical Association was formed, they took steps to save it. It was not rebuilt as accurately as it should have been and so the arms of the mill, which resembles the Dutch-type windmill, revolve only when the wind is west. However, they whirl merrily then and cornmeal is ground there and sold to tourists."

"It sounds fascinating," she said.

The old doctor smiled. "I'm certain you'll like Pirate Island and I have the feeling that Derek Mills will show you all the most important points of it."

She talked to the doctor for a while and then they parted. She went to an upper deck, braving a cold gale, for her first view of the island as it appeared on the horizon. Within a short time they were heading into Dark Harbor. She had an excellent chance to study the gray old village situated on a hill and also the dark granite cliffs nearby which had given the town its name. A hill rose high above Dark Harbor and she recognized this as Bald Mountain.

A group of people and a number of cars waited near the wharf as they docked. She went down to claim her own car and met the veteran doctor again.

He smiled at her and said, "You won't have far to drive. The Gray Heron is just up the hill on the left."

"Thank you," she said. And she saw that the cobblestone main street rose directly up from the wharf. The shops which lined it were mostly two and three story structures. The high-rise problem had not yet reached the island.

At last her car was ready and she drove away from the wharf and up the street which resembled something left over from an earlier era.

Ahead she saw the faded sign of the Gray Heron Hotel and parked her car. Then she got out and went up the steps leading to the plain doorway of the hotel office. Inside it smelled of rancid cigar smoke and stale cooking. There were a few hunting prints on the walls, some potted palms and cuspidors and a short desk which had been constructed across the doorway of another room in the rear.

A tallish man with a cruel, slab-face appeared behind the desk to greet her with a nod. "You have a reservation?" the man asked.

"Yes," she said. "My bags are still out in the car. My name is Jean Rivers."

The small, greedy eyes of the big man fixed on her. "You're the newspaper woman."

"I am," she said. "I think the paper made arrangements for my room."

"They did," he said, turning around an old-fashioned register. "Just sign right here."

She did so, noting that the most recent guest before her arrival had been a couple from New Jersey. She said, "Do you serve meals?"

"Only breakfast," the big man, whom she took to be Matt Kimble, said. "But there are plenty of restaurants around. One almost next door."

"I'll find them," she said. In her work she was used to being self-sufficient. Studying the big man's long, dour face, she thought of his strange history. She felt he might be cruel and not above a shady trick. Those small eyes were shifty. "You are Matthew Kimble?" she asked.

The big man nodded. "That's right. My family has had this place for years."

"So I've heard," she said. She glanced around the rather grimy, drably-painted lobby. "It has a very ancient air about it."

Matthew Kimble shrugged. "I haven't made any changes. People seem to like it this way. There's a tavern out the door on the right and ladies are welcome."

"Thank you, I'll remember that," she said. "Can you send out someone to help with my bags?"

"I don't have any porters," the big man said. "I'll help you with them."

And he did, carrying everything at one time. He had a bag in each hand and one wedged under his arm while she brought in a small overnight case. Her room was on the third floor and not too large. However, it seemed clean enough with maple furniture and checkered curtains and bedspread. One window looked down on the street and the other two had magnificent views of the harbor.

She went to the nearest window with a harbor view and drew the curtain aside to look out. The panorama of sparkling water, pleasure craft and ancient wharves was exciting. "I like this," she said.

Matthew Kimble put down her bags. "Bathroom is through that door," he said. "There's a shower but no tub."

"That will be all right," she said. She was going to tip him for helping with the bags but then refrained since he was the owner.

He hesitated by the door a moment. "You here for any special reason? You got a particular story in mind?"

"No," she said. "Not really. Have you any suggestions?"

The big man's slab face showed uneasiness. "No," he said hastily. "I just wondered."

He hurried on out and she stood gazing after him with a thoughtful smile. It struck her that Matt Kimble might be up to some illicit activity and that was why he'd been so interested. If there were any threat of exposure, he was looking for a warning.

She busied herself unpacking and then showered and dressed for her meeting with Derek Mills.

The stories she'd heard about the wealthy young man who made a career of taking care of the island's museum and historical sites had made her curious to meet him. The tragic illness of his wife had also aroused her sympathy.

She donned a chic green pants suit and went down to wait for Derek Mills. When she stepped inside the lobby, the first person she saw was a handsome, brown-haired young man in a plaid sports jacket and blue trousers. She at once decided this had to be him.

Going over to him with a smile, Jean said, "Are you by any chance Derek Mills?"

"I am," he said, returning her smile. "And you are Jean Rivers?"

"That's right," she laughed. "My boss sends you his warmest regards."

"Old Jeff," the young man said. "A good newspaperman. You must enjoy working with him."

"From time to time," she said, with a twinkle in her eyes. "He can have his difficult moments."

The tanned, even features of Derek Mills showed pleasure. "At any rate I'm delighted that he chose to have you come to Pirate Island."

"I'm sure I'm going to enjoy it."

He glanced at his watch. "I've booked dinner for us at a restaurant along the shore which I like. It closes rather early so if you're ready, perhaps we ought to get on our way."

"I'm ready to leave," she told him.

"Fine," he said, studying her with interest. "I somehow expected you'd be older and not so attractive."

"You're very kind," she said.

"I mean it," he said sincerely as they left the lobby of the

20

hotel for the street. "You have your car here?"

"Yes."

"You may as well leave it parked here and use mine," he told her. "It will be all right. So far we've avoided parking meters on the island."

She laughed. "A true haven."

He led her to a white convertible. The top was down and he said, "I'll put the top up. It's cool tonight and there's a breeze. The season has changed."

Settling on the leather seat beside him, she said, "There aren't too many convertibles on the road these days."

"This isn't mine," he confessed as he started the car. "I'm using it while mine is in for repair."

He backed the car out into the cobblestone street, headed up the hill, then took a right turn which led them to a shore route. As they drove along he began to relax and talk.

"You know something about the island?" he said.

"Some. I've read quite a few articles."

"I live along this road," he said. "And if you follow it out far enough, you'll come to the monastery that is a summer motel now. By the way, do you like where you are?"

"It has its drawbacks," she said. "But I don't mind it for a short stay. One excellent thing is that it is near the center of town."

"It is," Derek Mills said. "But if you decide that you'd prefer somewhere else, let me know and I'll do my best to locate you a nice place."

"Thanks. I'll stay where I am for the time being. By the way, the owner showed a special interest in what I'd come here to write about. I wondered if he's been up to anything illegal and is worrying about exposure."

"Ah, ha!" The young man at the wheel said. "Matt is a sly type. I hear he has been buying hijacked liquor and other stolen articles and selling them. He may be worried about that."

"So that's it," she said. "I assured him I had no special project in mind and he seemed a lot less worried."

They drove on and by the time they reached the restaurant its neon sign was bright against the darkness. He parked his car by it and they went in. As it was off season and getting late only about a dozen of the forty-odd tables in the big, softly-lighted dining room were filled.

The restaurant was done in country style with barn boards on the walls and great, rough oak beams at intervals on the ceiling. They were seated by a window overlooking the ocean and far in the distance she could see the beam of a lighthouse cutting across the black sky.

He noticed that she was studying the beam and said, "That's Gull Lighthouse. It's quite a few miles from here on Gull Point."

"I've read about it," she agreed.

They studied the menu and decided on boiled lobster. Derek also ordered cocktails. Over their drinks he smiled at her and said, "I suppose you can't wait to get started on some sensational story."

"I'm not all that anxious, though I can't waste any time," she said.

"There are so many stories to choose from here," he said. "It's hard to tell you where to begin."

"I know."

"I've arranged to have you meet Captain Zachary Miller tomorrow," he said. "I think he might be your best source of information."

"Dr. Taylor told me about him," she said. "I met the doctor on the boat and liked him."

"We think a lot of him here on the island," Derek said. "He attended my wife in the early stages of her illness."

"Really?" she said, pausing to see if he might add anything to this.

His handsome face shadowed. "But that is something else again," he said. "Our main business at the moment is to get you properly underway with your story."

She smiled. "Whatever the story may be."

His eyebrows raised. "According to Jeff you are looking for one of those ghost stories."

"If a suitable one comes along."

"The island, like all New England, has more than its share of them," he said. "But you'll want something of special interest. I think we can depend on the Captain to furnish the material."

"Have you spoken to him about me?"

"Yes. He's expecting you. He spends much of his time at the Pacific Club. It's off the main street and not far from your hotel. It was started years ago by a group of sea captains who chartered a ship to take them to New York to inspect the wonders of the famous *Great Eastern* steamship. They had such a fine time that they decided to organize a club when they returned. And it's gone on ever since. It's still difficult to become a member though you no longer have to be a sea captain."

"But Captain Miller is one?"

"Definitely. You're to have lunch there with him tomorrow and he'll spin you some tales afterward. There are several parlors in the club and he'll reserve one for your interview with him."

"That's very kind of you," she said.

"I told Jeff I'd do my best. I hope I'll be of some use and that I'll see you often during your stay here."

"I hope so, too," she said, feeling that he was at least as nice as people had said.

He paused and then abruptly changed the subject by telling her, "If you go along North Chester Street you'll find the Old North Cemetery. It is difficult to get to the various tombstones now because they are so overgrown with bayberry bushes and weeds. But there is a tombstone there that you will want to visit."

"Why?" she asked.

A weary smile crossed Derek's face. "You'll learn the reason when you talk with Captain Zachary Miller tomorrow. Two key figures in the story he will tell you are buried in the old cemetery. The stones are worn, but you can still read the names and dates. There is also the line, 'Repent my sins' in smaller lettering. Though it doesn't mention the sins, they included murder."

CHAPTER TWO

It seemed appropriate that when she awoke the next morning the fog had drifted in from the ocean to shroud the island in a heavy gray mist. Her evening with Derek Mills had been interesting and he'd regaled her with dozens of stories about the exciting history of Pirate Island. Today she would meet Captain Miller and hopefully get the basis for a feature article.

She went downstairs and found that breakfast was served in a corner of the tavern which did not open as a bar until noon. A waitress took her order and seemed to consider the extra work a nuisance. As Jean sat waiting to be served, Matt Kimble came lumbering in and paused by her table.

His small eyes studied her. "You being looked after?" he asked.

"The girl took my order," she said.

He grimaced. "She's slow! Don't expect it in a hurry. You can't get proper help these days. Lots of fog out today, do you mind it?"

"It's sort of fun," she said. "Gives everything a mysterious touch."

"Watch out if you do any driving," he warned her. "In these pea-soup fogs we generally rack up a few accidents."

"I'll remember," she promised.

The slab-faced man continued to study her suspiciously. "You and Derek Mills are writing something together?"

"No," she said. "I'm not doing a current story. I'm working on something about the past, preferably a ghost

25

story. Captain Miller is going to help me."

"Old Zachary?"

"Yes."

The big man looked less tense. "You stick to old Zachary and you won't go wrong. He knows this island like nobody else."

"So I've heard," she said.

"And put on your headlights when you're out in this fog," was his final advice before he moved on to vanish through the door to the kitchen area.

He must have chided the waitress because within a few minutes after his disappearance she came bearing a tray with bacon, eggs, orange juice, toast and coffee.

"It saves bother to bring it all at once," she informed Jean as she set the various items down.

The food was not first rate but Jean had learned to get along with ordinary breakfasts. When she finished she decided to stroll around the main street because of the fog. Had it been a fine day she would have driven about the island, but she didn't want to risk driving in the fog.

She visited a gift shop and found it too ordinary. Her next venture proved more interesting. This was a store devoted to marine needs, catering mostly to the pleasure-craft owners who came to the island but also storing supplies for the fishermen who lived in various tiny villages around the island. She spent some time talking to the owner and learned more of the island's story while doing so.

At twelve-thirty she made her way along the side street to the Pacific Club. A sad-faced, little old man answered the door with an inquisitive look as he saw her. He said, "What is your business, Miss?"

"I've come to meet someone."

The old man wore a white jacket and a black bowtie. He

was unimpressed. "Who?" he asked sourly.

"Captain Zachary Miller," she said, feeling somewhat uneasy. Standing there in the high-ceilinged vestibule with its glass-paneled doors was like being in another world—an older and more staid world.

The man's puckered face lost some of its annoyance. "Oh, you're the young woman come to visit the Captain," he said.

"That's right," she agreed.

"Come along," he told her and guided her in through a parlor to a small glass-enclosed verandah. And there seated alone in a big rocking chair was an elderly, balding man, fast asleep with a huge white angora cat in his lap.

"Captain!" the usher said loudly. The cat gave him an uneasy glance, nimbly leaped to the hardwood floor and vanished somewhere.

The captain opened his eyes and stared at Jean and the usher as if not yet awake. He had a lined, weathered face with strong features. She guessed that he must have been a dashing man in his day.

"Well?" he demanded irritably in a high-pitched voice.

"Your guest is here, Captain," the elderly usher told him.

"Guest?" his eyes opened wider and he raised himself from the chair.

"I'm Jean Rivers," she said. "Perhaps you've forgotten about my coming."

He raised a gnarled, protesting hand. "Of course I didn't," he declared. He gave the usher an annoyed glance. "It's just that he never tells me anything clearly. He's too old for his job and given to mumbling."

The usher looked shocked and angry. "That just isn't so, Captain! You were asleep."

"Asleep?" Captain Zachary Miller echoed with outrage. "I never sleep in the daytime. Sleeping is for the night. False

27

teeth, that's your problem, my man. You can't enunciate properly. Had a cook who suffered from the same trouble. Sacked him after the first voyage."

"Will you be having lunch now, Captain?" the usher said, ignoring this tirade as if he'd heard it all before.

"Yes," Captain Zachary Miller told him. "Myself and this young lady will be going to the dining room directly."

"I'll let them know," the usher said and he went on his way.

As soon as he was gone, Captain Miller smiled at her and said, "I'm sorry I nodded off before you arrived. Old man's failing, I fear. But I can't give him the satisfaction of knowing it."

She laughed. "I understand."

"The help are too old here and so are the members," Captain Zachary Miller said darkly. "In a sensible society most of them would be fed to the sharks. Still, I suppose when the truth is told I'm one of them." He beamed at her. "Delighted to see a young face."

He escorted her to a small dining room. On the way they passed through another parlor and she found herself the focus of attention from a half-dozen old gentlemen seated around the big room. Captain Zachary Miller held his ancient head high and offered them a smile of triumph.

When they reached their table, he confided, "It's not every day I have the pleasure of dining with a pretty girl."

"I feel like an intruder here," she said.

He chuckled. "You needn't. We get lady guests from time to time. Though they are rare at this season of the year. You're a nice novelty for the place."

Their table offered a view of the fogbound harbor, and for quite a while they had the dining room to themselves. A matronly woman acted as waitress and served them cocktails, which the captain insisted on, and a hearty dinner featuring roast beef and apple pie.

Over coffee the Captain said, "Well, that was most enjoyable. I get lonely eating by myself or with those old fellows every day."

"I suppose a change of company can be welcome."

"My wife died a while ago," he said. "Before that I only came here on an occasional afternoon. But now I come more often."

"That's natural," she said.

"So you're a friend of Derek Mills," the old captain said, studying her with interest.

"We only met last night but I had been told a lot about him."

"Fine young man," Captain Miller said. "Had more than his share of trouble but he's managed."

"So I understand," she said.

"He suggested I tell you the story of Madeline Renais," the captain went on. "He says you want a ghost feature for your paper."

"I do."

The captain smiled grimly. "Then that's the story for you. You see, Madeline Renais came back here to play the role of a ghost and avenge her own murder."

"It sounds as if it might be exactly what I want," she said enthusiastically.

"I won't try to tell you the story here," he said. "We'll move into one of the small private parlors. Then we won't be interrupted." He gave her a wink. "And we'll make those other old codgers wonder what we're up to."

Jean laughed. "I can see we're going to wind up the scandal of the Pacific Club."

"Place needs a scandal," Captain Zachary complained.

29

"Getting to be more like a geriatric center than anything else."

Having registered this opinion and finished his coffee he took her to a small parlor with bright floral wallpaper, Currier & Ives prints and wicker furniture. He closed the door so they would have privacy and had her sit in the most comfortable chair.

Then he began to pace back and forth. "The thing I have to do is decide where to begin my story. Because it didn't begin here on the island," he said.

"Oh?"

"No. It really started in Boston in 1894."

She took out a notebook and a pencil, ready to take down all he said in shorthand. She preferred this to using a tape recorder. She said, "You say it began in 1894?"

Captain Zachary Miller stood with his back to the fireplace and frowned as he searched his mind for the proper beginning. He said, "As I heard the story it began on a New Year's Eve in Boston in 1893. . . ."

The Tremont Street Musical Theatre, December 31, 1893. On the stage there was a special performance of the Moulin Rouge Revue headed by the Parisian star of song and dance, Mademoiselle Madeline Renais. Madeline, only a year away from her beloved Paris, was the toast of Boston. Her musical had been held over week after week and now she was doing this extra show to honor the approaching New Year.

Madeline, big red ostrich feather in her raven hair, wore a flowing crimson gown, which she lifted high in her cancan numbers to reveal her lovely legs. And on her engagement finger was the huge diamond given her by the man who had won her heart, Raymond Copeland, eldest son of a prominent Boston family. As she danced gaily before the packed theatre, every so often she lifted her eyes to the handsome blond man who sat in a box above the stage. Her glances, though brief, reflected all the adoration she felt for the Boston playboy.

Earlier that afternoon in her dressing room, she had been visited by Sam Elder, the squat, middle-aged, cigar-smoking manager of the Tremont Street Theatre and the revue. After her maid left them, the cynical Sam eyed her silently for a long moment.

Then taking his cigar from his thick lips he said, "I hear you're engaged to Raymond Copeland."

"So?" she said, staring into a hand mirror as she sat at her dressing table with her back partially turned to him.

"It's a mistake," Sam said gruffly.

"You would be bound to say that," she said, all assurance. She had learned to speak excellent English in her year of working in Boston and only slipped into an accent on stage.

The stout man shook his head. "Whatever I may be I'm honest when it comes to expressing my opinions. You should know that."

She gave him a wistful look. "But you are prejudiced in this. You know that Raymond wants me to leave the theatre and marry him. And I'm going to do it."

Sam Elder stared at her. "How can you be so blind?"

Her eyebrows lifted. "Blind?"

"Yes, blind," he repeated. "Blind to the kind of person Raymond Copeland is. He's a rich man's son who has never worked an honest day in his life."

She shrugged. "There has been no need for him to. And you are wrong. He does have an office in his father's bank."

The theatre manager gave a harsh laugh. "Which is

famous as a rendezvous for his drunken companions. He doesn't use it to work in."

"So he is a little wild," she said. "I'm sure he will change and drink less when we are married."

"You are wrong!" Sam Elder warned her. "He will probably wind up drinking more. You'll have lost your career in the theatre and then you'll lose your husband."

"No!" she said in protest and put the mirror down on the dresser. She stood up to face the squat man who was no taller than herself. "You are telling me lies to turn me against him."

He puffed on his cigar and eyed her in his calculating way. "Even if Raymond wanted to be a good husband to you, his family would never allow it."

"Why not?"

"Because they are the Brahmins of Boston. The Copelands are the oldest bankers in New England. The family ranks high in our social life. They will never allow a French music hall artist to become one of the family."

She lifted her chin. "They will have nothing to say about it."

"Don't trick yourself into believing that," Sam Elder said.

"I trust Raymond, he loves me. I'm sick of this life and I want to be his wife!"

Sam frowned and stared down at the floor. He lifted his eyes after a moment and in a tense voice said, "I had hoped not to tell you this. But I see that you need the ultimate warning. I have it on the soundest authority that several years ago Raymond Copeland was severely ill as the result of his dissipated life. He was given up by his doctors but confounded them by recovering suddenly. He seems cured, but his doctor assured me that the seed of his illness still remains in that young man. Would you want to marry someone who might become an invalid?"

Madeline listened with a look of disbelief. "You are making this story up. It has to be!"

"No—"

"I refuse to listen to you," she cried, turning away and putting her hands over her ears.

Sam Elder sighed. "So it appears you won't listen to reason."

"Not that kind of reason," she told him.

"I'm not saying these things out of selfishness, though it is true I don't want you to leave the theatre," he said. "I'm trying my best to give you good advice."

She gave him a bitter smile. "Thank you, Sam. I don't care to take it."

With that Sam Elder had spread his hands in a gesture of resignation and left the dressing room. She stood staring after him and feeling much more insecure than she might wish to admit. But she had given her heart to the handsome, reckless Raymond and though she knew she would miss the theatre she had agreed to give it up.

Now it was many hours later and she was finishing the last performance of the revue for the old year. Raymond was meeting her at the stage door and taking her to a New Year's party he was giving in a private salon of the Parker House. He had already given her a diamond and tonight he would officially announce their engagement to his many friends. She threw him a final smiling glance before she took her bows and left the stage to a roar of applause.

She lost no time changing from her stage costume to a low-cut evening gown. Marie, her personal maid, fussed with her hair. Finally everything suited her and, throwing a crimson cloak over her shoulders, she left the dressing room to hurry and meet Raymond.

On her way to the stage door she had to cross the stage

which was now in shadow with most of the lights out. Suddenly Sam Elder was standing in front of her. She halted on seeing him.

"You're in a great hurry," he said.

"I am. I'm meeting Raymond."

"He's talking to the stage doorman," Sam said matter-of-factly. "I saw him just now."

"Good."

The theatre owner eyed her soberly. "Have you thought over what I told you?"

"I have. I still feel the same."

"I'm sorry."

"So am I," she said. "I want us to remain friends."

He studied the glowing point of the cigar he held. "We shall always be that."

Madeline felt a sudden burst of emotion for the man who'd played such a major role in her career. She bent close to him and placing her hands on his shoulders kissed him gently.

"Goodnight, Sam," she said in a soft voice. "Happy New Year."

"Happy New Year," he said, not able to hide the sadness in his voice.

She quickly brushed by him and hurried to the stage door where a top-hatted and opera-cloaked Raymond and a gentleman friend were laughing and talking. On seeing her approach, Raymond turned, took her in his arms and kissed her many times.

"You're late, my dear," he said. "We mustn't keep our guests waiting!"

"I hurried," she told him.

"The sleigh is outside in the alley waiting to take us to the Parker House," the blond man said.

They left the theatre and stepped out into the winter cold. They bundled in the rear seat of the sleigh with a buffalo robe over them. The driver flicked his whip and the horses started off with their harness bells jingling and their hooves clattering over the icy cobblestones. They moved out onto Tremont Street with its crowds of late merrymakers, past the glowing amber gas lamps on every corner, by the Common with its expanse of white snow and to the noble brick structure of the Parker House.

In the private salon of the ancient hostelry the party was already under way. Raymond had hired a small orchestra for music and dancing. A long white table at one end of the big room was laden with food delicacies and great magnums of champagne on ice. White-capped chefs were there to serve the nearly fifty guests.

At the appearance of Raymond and Madeline, there was cheering in the room. Men in white ties and tails and women in evening gowns danced around them. Raymond stood with her in the middle of it all, his handsome face glowing with delight. He'd already had a good deal to drink and now he advanced to the table for champagne.

At his side Madeline said, "Not too much! The New Year will soon be here."

"I'll manage nicely," he promised her as he helped himself to the champagne.

A few minutes before the New Year would arrive, Raymond took her through the french doors to a balcony. He closed the door behind them to shut out the revelry and placed an arm around her. The air was cold and she pressed close to him, willing to endure the icy chill to be alone with him at this most important moment of the year.

She gazed down at Tremont Street far below them and the white vastness of the Common and the Public Gardens beyond. Then from across the street, where the snow-draped church steeple rose high against the star-studded sky, there came the crystal sound of chimes. And the chimes were echoed by other bells from nearby churches, as joyous shouting came up from the street at the arrival of the New Year.

Raymond took her in his arms and pressed his lips to hers. He held her this way until the clamor was at its height. Then they rejoined their friends and the hilarity inside. The orchestra played and she and Raymond whirled around in a lively waltz with the others.

After all this, his announcement of their engagement came as an anti-climax. Some of the guests had already left and others had drunk too much to be fully aware of what was being said. It was an omen which she chose to ignore.

Later when Raymond took her home to her own hotel room, he told her, "Next week I want you to come to Brookline and live with my family until we are married."

She shook her head. "I don't think I'd be happy."

"Nonsense! Of course you will," Raymond said in his overbearing fashion. "I want you to get to know each other before the wedding."

Madeline hesitated, all her happiness draining away. "Please don't make me do it."

"You will do it," he said, ignoring her plea. "My grandmother Martha will welcome you. And as for the others, I couldn't care less how they feel. They'll come around to accepting you."

She glumly listened to his prediction and prayed that he'd either forget about his plan or change his mind. So she argued no more but kissed him a final goodnight.

Unhappily he had no intention of changing his plan. And so one evening ten days later she found herself in a bedroom of the Copeland family mansion in Brookline. Raymond had moved her there bag and baggage. She knew she could be grateful to him for his belief in her and this demonstration that he intended to marry her. But she couldn't be happy about it. It seemed to her that he was forcing her on the family and she was not in any position to defend herself.

The bedroom in which he had installed her was elegant like the rest of the old mansion. Yet she was truly terrified. Her whole life had been dedicated to the stage and when she was away from it she always found herself ill at ease. This occasion was no exception.

She was dressed in a dark green gown and ready for Raymond to take her down to meet the others at dinner. She was more nervous than she had been before any audience. As she paced back and forth before the blazing logs in the room's fireplace there was a knock on the door.

Madeline started nervously at the sound of it. Then she rather timidly went and opened it. Raymond was standing there in a formal, black suit. He entered the room and told her, "My grandmother Martha wants to meet you. She's an invalid so she won't be down to dinner. We have just time to give her a few minutes."

"Are you sure?" she worried.

"Of course I am," he said in his brash way. And he smilingly led her from her room and down the stairs to the floor below. He guided her along a wide hallway until they came to an open door of a large bed-sitting room. There ensconced in a large easy chair sat a frail-looking old woman with a silver-headed cane in her hand.

"Well, Raymond, you've fetched her!" the old woman said with a smile on her thin face and she tapped the floor happily with her cane.

"This is Madeline Renais, Grandmother," Raymond said.

The old woman had sparkling, amazingly young blue eyes in her thin lined face. Her hair was white and piled up in a pompadour. She held out a frail hand towards Madeline and said, "Come here, my dear, I won't bite you!"

"Good evening," Madeline said hesitantly, as she knelt before the old woman.

Martha Copeland patted her tenderly on the head. "What a lovely child you are! I thought being an actress would have spoiled you but I see that it hasn't."

"That's what I tell the others," Raymond said in an irate voice. "But they refuse to believe me."

"She will make them believe," his grandmother said with approval. She turned to Madeline again to say, "You must forgive me for not standing. Some years ago I broke my hip and it has left me a helpless invalid."

"You do manage to get about some," Raymond corrected her.

The old woman tapped her cane again. "Always one of your bad habits, Raymond. You always have argued with me. I get around with great pain so I have gradually cut down on my movements."

"It was nice of you to want to see me," she faltered.

"Nonsense! It is you who have done me the favor, dear child," the old woman said.

She gazed around her. "It is such a big place it frightens me," she said.

Raymond's grandmother laughed. "I remember well when I first saw it I felt the same way. I was a poor girl in Philadelphia. But I had a good family line. Trent Copeland was there on banking business and I met him at a party given by a wealthy uncle. He fell in love with me and I had no chance to stop him. He was that sort of person. When I first came here I was a frightened little thing like you. Now I'm the matriarch of the household. Life is short and plays strange tricks on us!"

"Thank you for telling me the story. It gives me courage," Madeline told the old woman.

"Exactly what I wanted to do," Martha Copeland said. "And someday you must come and dance for me up here."

She smiled. "I'll be glad to."

The old woman waved her hand in dismissal. "Now go on downstairs with Raymond and greet the others. And don't let them frighten you. Remember I was mother to Thomas and am grandmother to the others."

"I will," she promised and she kissed the old woman on the cheek before leaving her.

As she and Raymond started downstairs she said, "Your grandmother is a charming and kind person."

"I couldn't agree more," Raymond said, smiling and swaying a little.

To her dismay she saw that he'd been drinking too much. She told him, "You've had a lot to drink."

He eyed her happily. "I had to bolster my courage, too. Let us proceed."

It was the start of a long series of unhappy moments she was to experience that first evening in the Brookline mansion. Raymond guided her into the parlor with its great chandeliers where his widower-father greeted them coldly. She saw at once that Thomas Copeland had inherited none of his mother's warmth. He had evidently taken after his stern father.

After Raymond introduced her to his father, the elder Copeland eyed her rather icily and said, "Have you had any previous marriages, Miss Renais?"

"No," she said at once. "I was sure Raymond must have told you my history."

"Sorry, didn't get around to it," her blond fiancé apologized.

His father, an erect, gray-haired patrician, gave him a grim glance. In his clipped Boston manner, he said, "My son is given to impulsive actions, Miss Renais. This is not the first time he has become involved with a woman in the theatre, but it does happen to be the first time he's announced his engagement to any of his conquests."

She felt her cheeks burn. "I wasn't aware I was one of a company until this moment," she said. Turning to Raymond, she inquired, "What have you to say to that?"

Raymond was looking angry. He exclaimed, "My father is a cold fish. You mustn't feel badly about anything he says."

Thomas Copeland's face was flushed. He said, "My son has no respect for me, as you can judge for yourself."

"Come along," Raymond said harshly, taking her almost roughly by the arm. "I want you to meet the rest of the menagerie!"

"Please don't say such things," she begged in a low voice.

"Who cares?" he scoffed drunkenly.

"I do," she said in a low whisper.

The next person she met was Raymond's younger brother, James. James Copeland was simply a junior edition of his stern father. He had a small mustache and the commanding manner of a banker. His interest in her seemed to be mostly financial.

He said, "I hear that you have had a most successful year in Boston after starring in Paris."

"Yes," she said.

The young Jim Copeland studied her coldly. "Then you must have earned a great deal. You have to be wealthy."

"I regret that I'm not," she said.

"Why not?" He shot at her, making it sound as if she were guilty of great negligence.

"I have not been a star all that long," she said. "And being a star is very expensive."

"Ah! You have been extravagant," Jim Copeland said.

At this moment he was joined by his wife, Alice. She was a big woman, somewhat overweight. She had once been pretty but now her face had taken on a pouting expression.

Alice Copeland's opening gambit was, "How thin you are! I suppose it must be the exercise. Dancing on the stage in all those ridiculous outfits."

"I never thought of them as being ridiculous," she told the stout young woman.

"I have attended the theatre only occasionally," Alice said with dignity. "But my mother always told me all theatre people are immoral."

"To about the same degree as those not on the stage," was Madeline's reply.

Raymond roared so with drunken gaiety at this sally that whatever cleverness she felt her answer had possessed was spoiled for her. Clearly none of the family thus far, with the exception of his grandmother, had been at all considerate of her. And there was more to come.

Raymond piloted her across the room where a lovely blonde girl who resembled him enough to be his twin was standing in the company of a pleasant, brown-haired young man. As Raymond and Madeline approached them, she could see the girl prepare herself for the introductions which followed.

Juliet was Raymond's sister, and the young man at her side was her fiancé, Hudson Strout. Juliet said, "I see you've been drinking too much, Raymond."

Raymond made an expansive gesture. "My usual amount!"

"Meaning a little beyond your capacity," Juliet said with a

grim smile. And she asked Madeline, "Has he ever been sober since you've met?"

She was startled by the question. "Of course he has been. Many times."

"I wondered about it," Juliet said too sweetly. "I can picture him carrying on his entire courtship in a drunken state. It makes it easier to understand."

Before Madeline could reply to this, Hudson Strout drew her aside and said quietly, "You mustn't take all this too seriously. They are as nervous as you are and not too responsible."

"Thank you for trying to help," she said.

"I'm a lawyer, it's my duty to counsel," he said with a friendly smile. "I saw your show many times and I think you are extremely talented."

"Hudson," Juliet called to her fiancé reprovingly. And with an embarrassed look he excused himself and went to join her.

Raymond smiled drunkenly at Juliet and said, "Well, how do you like them?"

"I think it more to be considered how they like me," she said.

He gave an expansive wave of his arm. "They think you're wonderful."

She looked at him and said bitterly, "I promise you that any one of them would be delighted to kill me!" At that moment she had no idea how true her words were.

CHAPTER THREE

That first evening at the Copeland mansion in Brookline was only the beginning of Madeline Renais' ordeal with the aristocratic Boston family. Each succeeding day she was made to feel more like an intruder and was snubbed by everyone but her husband-to-be and old Martha Copeland. Had it not been for Raymond's grandmother, she would have fled the cold atmosphere of the great brick house.

Raymond spent a great deal of his time in the city. He told Madeline it had to do with the banking business. But many times he returned intoxicated, and there were nights when he did not come back to the family mansion at all. He was always quick to offer her a plausible excuse for these lapses and because she really loved him she was perhaps too ready to forgive him.

But one evening when they had the small parlor to themselves, before the blazing hearth, she kneeled on the floor by his chair, she begged him to let her leave the house and take a room in a downtown hotel.

"They all resent me," she said on the brink of tears. "I'll never be happy here."

Raymond's handsome face was troubled. "Nonsense," he said. "It just takes time to know them and for them to understand you."

"It won't happen."

"I say it will," he insisted. "We'll be married in a few weeks. Meanwhile it is more convenient to have you here. There are the fittings for your wedding wardrobe and all the other planning."

"I could do all that in a hotel," she persisted.

"You could, but it is much better this way," Raymond said. "To outsiders it will appear that my family has taken you to their bosom and that will be important in how you are accepted by others in our social circle."

She stared at him. "But that is like perpetrating a fraud," she exclaimed. "They haven't accepted me!"

"People will assume they have," Raymond said, a trace of a smile replacing his former concern. "And that will be good for you." He paused for a moment. "You see my own reputation isn't above reproach. I've been the black sheep of the family and I need some whitewashing as well."

"And as long as my staying here serves your purpose, you don't care how miserable I am?" she said unhappily. "I'm beginning to think I should never have left the theatre."

He quickly bent down and kissed her gently on the lips. Then taking her hands in his, he told her, "You mustn't ever say that. Nor must you doubt my love for you."

Her eyes mirrored her concern. "Sometimes I wonder."

"You needn't," he said. "In no time we'll be married and then we'll go on a honeymoon trip. I've been thinking of Italy."

She brightened. "I would love that. Once I toured in Italy. I know all the cities. What fun it would be to do them together!"

"If all goes well, we shall," he said.

"And when we return?"

He hesitated. "What about it?"

"Where are we going to live? Surely not here!"

Raymond hedged for a moment. "There is plenty of room in this house."

"No!" she protested. "Never! I will not begin our married life here!"

"Very well," he said, holding her hands tightly in his. "I will find a place. And tomorrow night I'm taking you to dine at Loch-Ober's and afterward we are invited to a party."

She listened to his plans for the next night with a deep feeling of uneasiness. She was worried that he was emphasizing them to take her mind off the future. She meant to talk to him about a house again and make him understand she would not go on living with his family. Not only did their cold attitude offend her but she was actually afraid of the dark old mansion.

Often when she woke up in the night she thought she heard footsteps in the corridor outside her room. And once she had sat up in bed in stark terror at the sound of the doorknob being slowly turned. She had stared at the door through the darkness waiting for what might come next, but the knob had been released and she'd heard the footsteps outside fading away.

She'd mentioned these incidents to Raymond and he had laughed at her fears. She then took them to the only other person in the big house to whom she could turn, his grandmother. One afternoon when she was up keeping the invalid matriarch of the Copeland family company, she'd broached the subject.

Martha Copeland listened to her account of the ghostly events with a sober look and said, "You must be careful. Especially in the dark. Things do happen which are hard to explain."

She stared at her and asked, "Are you saying that this house is haunted?"

Raymond's grandmother clutched the arms of her chair with veined hands and said, "I'm merely telling you it is not a happy house. I prefer to say no more than that."

"I feel frightened here," Madeline admitted. "And my

fears have increased lately. It is as if there is some unknown threat which I do not understand—danger stalking me of which I'm not aware."

"Then you should listen to that inner voice of warning," Martha Copeland said. "I know I would."

She gave the invalid an anxious glance. "I've never known this kind of fear before. And Raymond just laughs when I tell him."

"Raymond is a handsome young man and my favorite, I suppose," his grandmother sighed. "But he is not what one might term a sensitive person."

"He surely is not," she agreed bitterly.

"So you cannot count on him."

"You are the only other person in this house whom I can talk to," she lamented.

"What about Juliet?" the old woman asked.

"She hates me. She is even miserable towards me when her fiancé is around to hear."

"Ah!" the old woman said. "I can believe that. She is very jealous of Hudson. Juliet, for all her good looks, is a very insecure person. She was as a little girl and she hasn't changed."

"I have no interest in her fiancé," she said. "Though he has been more considerate to me than anyone else."

"Hudson is a fine person," Martha agreed. "I hope that Juliet makes him happy. I'm afraid I rather doubt it. She has never known how to savor life herself."

"I'll be glad when I'm married and can get away from here," she said.

The old woman gave her a sad smile. "Then I shall miss you. I enjoy our talks and your stories about the theatre."

"I like being with you," she said, touched by the old woman's sincerity.

"I wish it were summer and we were at our place in Dark

Harbor," Martha Copeland said. "You might find it more pleasant there."

"Dark Harbor?" The name was unknown to her.

"Yes," Martha said. "It is a town on Pirate Island. The island is located off Cape Cod. One takes a train to the Cape and then a steamer across to the island. It is my favorite spot. My husband built me a house there which we call Pinecrest."

"It sounds pleasant," she said.

"It is an old house now," the invalid said. "But much newer than this one. And there one can go outside and enjoy the lawns and the refreshing salt air."

"I can tell that you like it," Madeline said.

"My son, Thomas, has wanted to sell it," the old woman went on. "But I have refused to allow it."

"Does Raymond like it? He has never spoken to me about it."

Martha Copeland smiled sadly. "That doesn't surprise me. My grandson thinks more of his wild parties and drinking than of the simple family existence at Dark Harbor. Yet as a boy he used to enjoy it there. He often went sailing."

"I must ask him about it," she said. "There are so many things about the family I don't know."

The old woman in the armchair gave her a rather strange look and said, "Perhaps that is fortunate in some ways."

Madeline later spoke of Dark Harbor to Raymond but he showed no interest. He was recovering from a late night party which he'd attended alone and was impatient with any serious talk.

"I have a dreadful headache," he told her as they stood together in the elegant living room.

"You drink too much," she reproached him.

His manner became cold. "I dislike your criticizing my personal habits," he said. "I have to put up with enough of

47

that from the rest of the family."

"They mean it for your good," she insisted.

His handsome face was marred by a nervous tic in his cheek which she had seen many times before when he was tense. He clenched his hands as he said, "I will not be preached to by them or by you. Please understand that!" And he stalked out of the room leaving her standing alone and distressed.

It was early evening and she had looked forward to a quiet hour or two with him. But as she stood there she heard the front door open and close as Raymond left the house. It was a favorite trick of his whenever she took him to task about anything.

She was about to leave the room when she heard a movement behind her and turned to see Raymond's father standing there with a grim look on his patrician face. She had not been aware that he was in the room and at once wondered if he had heard the quarrel.

This question was answered for her immediately when Thomas Copeland said, "I heard your exchange with my son."

"Oh?" She thought it mean that he should have been lurking in the background spying on them.

The austere, gray-haired man was studying her closely. He said, "Surely you must realize by now that your engagement to Raymond is a mistake."

Defensively, she said, "Why do you say that?"

"It's obvious!" he said with undisguised disgust. "I didn't have to hear you just now to be aware of it. You two will never get along."

"It will be different after we are married!"

Thomas Copeland scoffed. "It will be worse!"

"How can you say that?"

"I know my son!"

"You're not being fair!"

The grim-faced widower took a step nearer her. "You have too many problems to overcome. Your lack of a social position and Raymond's wildness. You should admit defeat and give it up now. Go back to the theatre!"

She gazed at him with angry eyes. "You'd like that, wouldn't you? None of you think I'm good enough for Raymond."

Thomas Copeland smiled thinly. "Let us say you have not had a suitable background."

"You don't realize that because of that I might be better for him than one of your Boston society girls," she said unhappily. "I have given up a wonderful career to be his wife!"

The gray-haired man nodded. "I understand that. And I'd even be willing to pay you a substantial sum to get you started in the theatre again if you'd break this ill-starred engagement."

Her eyes widened. "You are offering to pay me off?"

"I wouldn't phrase it that way," he said with his banker's suaveness.

"But that is what it amounts to!"

"Look at it any way you like," he said.

"I'm sorry. I'm not interested," she told him.

"I see," he said quietly. "Do you mind if I tell you I think you are a fool?"

"Your opinions don't matter to me!" she retorted.

"If you remain here you may find yourself in great danger," Thomas Copeland warned her. And having said this he left the room.

She was stunned by his cryptic warning. She did not know what to make of it. Was it possible that he was personally threatening her? Had those sounds in the midnight hours anything to do with what he'd said? Had it been his hand that had turned the knob of her bedroom door?

Her uneasiness in the old mansion grew, and she watched the others with new suspicion. Juliet did everything she could to avoid her. It was only on rare occasions that they exchanged a few words.

As for Raymond's brother, James, and his wife, Alice, they always gave the impression that they'd been secretly plotting against her. Whenever she would come upon them suddenly, they would freeze and fall silent. When they did talk to her it was in a most impersonal way.

Once the stout Alice had informed her, "You know that James is his father's favorite."

"He and his father are much alike," she'd said.

Alice smiled maliciously as she said, "You mustn't expect Raymond to be given any important role in the family business. His father doesn't trust him as he does my husband."

"That's not important to me," she told her prospective sister-in-law.

"It could affect you a great deal financially," Alice said with pleased spitefulness. "Raymond will only have what his father leaves him. He'll not earn anything from the bank, and at the rate he spends money he could soon wind up a pauper."

"I'm not worried about that," she said. "I have always been able to earn a good living."

"Then why would you want to marry someone like Raymond?" Alice wanted to know.

"I think I needn't answer that," she told Alice, turning her back on her.

The atmosphere in the old Brookline mansion did not get any friendlier. As the time for her wedding to Raymond neared, Madeline found herself with some necessary errands to look after. She was grateful for the opportunity to get away from the grim household. Raymond arranged for a livery sleigh to call for her and take her to downtown Boston.

It was her custom to remain downtown for the afternoon and shop. She always had her noon meal in one of the several good eating places and usually patronized the famous Parker House dining room.

One noon in mid-February when she was in Boston on one of these shopping expeditions she engaged a table at the Parker House as usual. She had asked Raymond to join her for lunch, but he had pleaded other business. She privately worried that he preferred to dine with those who would not reprimand him for his heavy midday drinking as he knew she would.

The day was cold and as she took her place at the table the headwaiter helped her off with her warm, fur-trimmed coat. She removed her gloves and sat back to look at the menu. The room about her was beginning to fill with noonday customers.

The headwaiter stood by respectfully and commented, "We have missed you in the theatre, Miss Renais."

She glanced up from the menu with a smile. "Thank you. I have missed being in the shows."

"Do you plan to return?"

"I think not," she said.

"A great pity," the headwaiter told her. "May I recommend the scrod for today?"

"Fine," she said. "It is always good here."

He went away to give her order to the waiter and she sat back to observe the room. Most of the customers were male executives. She knew that Sam Elder sometimes had lunch there and rather wistfully hoped to see his ugly, yet somehow attractive face, once again. She knew that he had found it hard to forgive her for leaving his theatre.

Suddenly a figure halted by the table and bowed to her. She saw that it was the lawyer, Hudson Strout, Juliet's fiancé.

"Hello, Miss Renais," the young man said in a friendly tone.

"How nice to see you," she said.

He indicated the empty chair at her table. "May I sit down for just a moment?" he asked. "I'm meeting a client here and he has not arrived yet."

"Please do," she said.

The pleasant young man said, "You're looking very attractive today. Where is Raymond?"

"I don't know."

"He should be here."

She looked down at her plate. "He seemed to think not. I'm doing some important shopping. He can't abide the stores."

Hudson Strout laughed. "Few men can unless they are shopping for themselves."

She smiled. "I'm afraid that is all too true. I haven't seen you at the house lately."

The young lawyer showed some embarrassment. "No. I've been extremely busy and out of the city a great deal. I doubt that Juliet misses me."

"I'm certain that she must," Madeline said.

Hudson Strout looked at her earnestly. "Let me say, Miss Renais, that I do not always see eye to eye with Juliet."

"That is not so surprising."

"Especially in some things," he went on. "The way the Copeland family has treated you, to speak plainly. I consider it an outrage."

She felt her cheeks burn. "Please," she said. "I do not think it is a thing we should discuss."

"I'm sorry," he said. "I did not mean to embarrass you but I feel deeply about it."

"Thank you," she said.

His brown eyes met hers. "You are a young woman of great talent and I think *you* are making the sacrifice in marrying Raymond. It is incredible that his family should think to the contrary."

She offered him a melancholy smile. "Points of view can be very different."

"That is surely true or the Copelands would be giving you your just due," the handsome young lawyer said.

"You are very kind," she said. "But if you offer such sentiments to your Juliet I'm sure you'll really have an argument."

"We already have," he confessed. "That is why I have not been visiting her. I hope to teach her a lesson."

Madeline felt some dismay at hearing this. "Please don't cause yourself trouble on my account."

The young man across the table from her said, "Anything I may have said was not solely on your account but for my own integrity. I have certain standards of conduct, Miss Renais, and I refuse to accept deceit."

"That is very noble of you," she said. "I only hope that you may be able to live up to your credo and keep Juliet as your fiancé."

"Better that we resolve our differences now than later," he said. "And I think you should consider that. Are you certain you and Raymond can have a happy marriage?"

Before she could make any reply to this, a third party came to stand by their table. It was Sam Elder, resplendent in a long dark winter coat and carrying a black homburg in his hand. His ugly, squarish face displayed grim humor.

"Well, Madeline, I find you in good company," the theatre manager said.

Hudson Strout rose at once and said, "Of course you wouldn't realize that I know Miss Renais. I've met her at the Copelands."

Sam Elder smiled. "Interesting," he said. And he asked her, "Are you enjoying your retirement from the theatre?"

"I haven't decided yet," she said evasively. "There hasn't really been enough time."

Sam Elder nodded. "I'll be interested in hearing what you have to say a year from now. I imagine the wedding will be soon?"

"Yes, in a few weeks."

"My congratulations," the squat man said.

"Thank you," she replied. It was the first time he had ever congratulated her on her marriage.

Sam Elder smiled at Hudson Strout and said, "I must explain that Hudson is my lawyer."

The young man nodded. "Yes. Mr. Elder is the client whom I've been waiting for."

She managed a small smile. "I'm glad to know you are friends and business associates."

Sam Elder eyed her mockingly. "I trust you won't forget your old friends when you become Mrs. Raymond Copeland."

She blushed. "Of course I won't."

The theatre manager turned to Hudson Strout again. "If you don't mind I'd like to order dinner at once and get down to business while we eat. I have a busy day ahead of me."

"Of course," Hudson Strout said, and he bowed to her. "You will excuse us, Miss Renais."

"Don't let me keep you from your work," she said. "It has been most pleasant meeting you both."

The two men moved on to a table at the other end of the room. The waiter came with her scrod and she gave it her attention. She finished her dinner while Sam Elder and Hudson Strout were still at their table. Neither of them noticed her as she left the restaurant.

The meeting with Sam Elder had been somewhat of an embarrassment because of the ill-feeling when she left his theatre. But he seemed to have recovered from his anger. And she decided it probably had been a good thing that they had met in this way. It would make any other meetings easier.

She'd had no idea that Hudson Strout was his lawyer. Her talk with the young man had been most enlightening. She felt that she had found another friend. At the same time she was certain that Juliet must be enraged at her fiancé's championing her. It created a most awkward situation. She had not paid too much attention to the young lawyer at their earlier meetings, but now she felt that he was a rather special young man. She could not help but be impressed by his high ethics and his sincere manner. She only wished that Raymond might be more like him.

She finished her shopping and went to wait for the sleigh. The livery stable from which Raymond rented it was most reliable and the vehicle appeared in front of Filene's exactly at five. It had begun to snow and Madeline was anxious to get home with her packages.

The sleigh took the route along Beacon Street and made good time. But when she reached the mansion there was bad news.

Raymond's thin, sour brother James broke it to her. "My grandmother is ill."

She was startled. "It must have been sudden."

"It was," the young man said. "The doctor just left. He says it is pneumonia."

"How awful!" she exclaimed. "Is there anything I can do?"

"No," James said in his acid way. "We have a trained nurse. Grandmother is in a delirium and doesn't seem to recognize anyone."

"I hope she recovers," Madeline said.

"The doctor thinks there is a good chance she will," James replied. "So all we can do now is wait."

"I'm so sorry," she said.

James gave her a cold glance. "I can't see that she would be that important to you. You're not one of the family yet."

She felt the pain of his sarcasm, but refused to show her feelings. Instead, she said, "Your grandmother has been a good friend to me."

"Really?" James said superciliously.

She hurried on upstairs, anxious to get away from him. The manner in which he aped the cold airs of his father was disgusting to her. She liked his wife Alice even less than she did James. They were well-suited to each other in their lack of grace.

A lamp had been lit and set out on her dresser. She entered the privacy of her bedroom with a feeling of relief. After she put away her purchases, she washed and changed into a gown for dinner. As she fixed her hair in the mirror, she began to worry about Raymond and hope that he would arrive home sober. It would be a disgrace if anything happened to his grandmother while he was away carousing.

She made her way down the shadowed stairs and was relieved to hear Raymond's voice issuing from the living room with that of his father. He sounded sober if somewhat concerned, and she went in to join the two men.

Raymond turned as she entered the room and came to greet her. "You finished your shopping in good time," her fiancé said.

"Yes," she said, with a small smile. "I had a good day in the stores."

"I can imagine that it cost a penny," her husband-to-be said.

"I find that most worthwhile things in life can be expensive," was her reply.

"You've heard about my grandmother?" he asked.

"Yes," she said, ignoring his father for a moment to get a few words with him. "I'm so glad you're here."

His handsome face showed annoyance. "Just what does that mean? Why shouldn't I be here?"

"I meant to say that occasionally you arrive home much later," she said.

"Indeed?" he gave her an annoyed look.

"I didn't mean to make you angry," she apologized.

"You surely go about it the right way," was Raymond's reply. He turned to his father now and said, "You're certain the doctor said Grandmother was to have no visitors in her room?"

"Yes," Thomas Copeland said. "And I must insist that his wishes in that regard be carried out." Then he turned on his heel and left them alone.

She gave Raymond an unhappy look. "If anything happens to your grandmother no one will miss her more than I," she said.

"You have become that fond of her?"

"Yes. I don't think this house will be bearable for me without her."

Raymond's handsome face took on an overbearing smile. "I'm sure that you'll survive."

"You don't really understand how I feel," she told him anxiously. "There is more to it than the snubs I've taken from your family."

"Oh?"

"Yes," she said, following it up now that she'd begun. "I'm actually afraid of this dark old house!"

"Afraid?" he asked with an air of disbelief.

"Yes," she insisted. "It's hard to explain. But much of the time I feel menaced by something. I don't know what, but I'm aware of its threat. I find myself hesitating in the darkness for fear I may stumble on some horror, and at nights I hear sounds in the corridors. And sometimes the handle of my bedroom door is turned!"

"My!" Raymond said mockingly. "You have a regular torrent of woes!"

"And none of them made more easy by your drinking!"

The handsome blond man laughed easily. "What a strange way to react to Grandmother's illness! Instead of grief you show anger at me. You betray your lowly French background by your quarreling with me like a fishwife!"

It was too much! The last straw! She lashed out at him with her fists and sobbed at the same time. He caught her hands and held them, enjoying her frustration.

Then he said, "I'm sorry. I oughtn't to have said that. I, too, am upset. Please forgive me!"

It was typical of her caring for him that she could quickly get over her anguish and accept his apology. He touched his silk handkerchief to her eyes to dry her tears and murmured soothing words to her. Then as he returned the handkerchief to his upper jacket pocket he bent close to her and gave her a kiss.

"So the tempest is over," he said with a sigh. "We are all overwrought. Come, let us join the others at dinner."

Dinner was always a difficult time for her. And on this night of sorrow it was even more trying. The conversation at the table was stilted and cold. She saw Juliet studying her with a malicious look of satisfaction. And she was sure that Raymond's sister had observed her red eyes and knew that she'd been crying. The others were too self-centered to notice anything.

The doctor returned soon after dinner and ascended the stairway to the upper apartment occupied by the sick old woman. A pall of gloom hung over the house as she and Raymond waited with the others in the living room. Only Thomas Copeland had accompanied the doctor to the sickroom.

Raymond went to the window, drew aside the drape and gazed out. His handsome face seemed unusually pale and the nerve in his cheek was twitching once again. He said, "The snow is falling heavily. We are having a true storm."

"It was just starting when the sleigh picked me up at Filene's," she said.

He allowed the drape to fall back in place as he turned to her. "I feel ill," he said. "A sudden dizziness. It has been a strenuous day. If you'll excuse me I think I'll go to my room."

She was at once concerned. "Perhaps you should consult the doctor before he leaves?"

"No," Raymond said. "That's not necessary. I've had these spells before. They date back to my old illness. All I need is rest. I have a sleeping draught in my room and that will look after this thing."

"You're certain?" she worried.

"Quite certain," he said. "I'll inquire about grandmother on my way up to my room." He kissed her and quickly made his way from the living room.

Juliet came over to her and asked, "Where is he going?"

"To his room," she said. "He has complained of a headache and not feeling well."

"Oh," the other girl said and moved away from her again.

James and Alice were standing at the far end of the big room from her. She could see them with their heads together, talking in low tones. Once again she had the conviction that they were conspiring against her. She remained by the window waiting for Thomas Copeland to come down with the doctor.

They returned a few minutes later. The gray-haired patrician saw the doctor out and then returned to the living room to announce, "There is no change. The doctor thinks that she is weathering the crisis well but it will be a few days before we'll know if she is going to live or die."

She went over to him. "Now that I've heard the word I'll go to bed. Raymond has already gone upstairs. He was feeling ill."

Thomas stared at her oddly. "Yes I know. I spoke with him."

"He said he would stop by on his way," she recalled. "I hope your mother recovers."

"Thank you," Thomas Copeland said coldly. He kept staring at her in that same strange fashion as if he had more to say but couldn't bring himself to speak.

She stood there before him a moment longer, puzzled by his odd manner. Then as she mounted the dimly-lighted stairs and made her way along the dark corridor to her room, the same fears that had tormented her at other times returned.

Reaching her bedroom, she quickly went inside. She told herself that her fears were groundless, but this made them no less terrifying. Knowing that Raymond was ill made her feel more vulnerable and alone as she prepared for bed.

When it came time to extinguish the single lamp in her bedroom she began to tremble. But refusing to give in to childish fears, she put the lamp out and left the room in darkness. Then she got into bed and drew the covers over her. The heavy snowfall had made the night strangely still and now she lay staring up into the black shadows listening for those eerie night sounds.

CHAPTER FOUR

She had no idea how long she slept. But she suddenly came awake with a feeling of utter terror. She sat up in bed staring into the dark shadows of her bedroom. She had a sensation that someone else was in the room. Memories of those other times when she'd heard creaking floor boards in the corridor outside her door and the door handle had been slowly turned flooded back to her!

Had someone managed to enter her room while she was asleep? It was a terrifying possibility. She pulled the bedclothes up around her. The logs in the fireplace had burned out and the room was cold. The conviction that she was not alone still nagged at her. She scanned the dark room as best she could, but there seemed to be no one lurking in the shadows.

Then she heard the breathing and her heart almost stopped! The heavy breathing of someone close by the bed! She stared into the blackness apprehensively and all at once saw the outline of the intruder in the darkness. She gasped at the sight of the black hooded figure with slitted eyeholes. The apparition moved closer to her and she screamed.

Only one scream escaped her lips and then strong hands seized her throat as her attacker began to throttle her. She tried vainly to fight back but to little avail. The crushing hands continued their brutal task. Soon she was unconscious and the cold darkness pressed in on her. . . .

She listened to the sound of low moaning in the distance,

then it ceased and she heard a mad voice gibbering and chuckling. Her head was aching fearfully and she was finding it difficult to breathe.

She lifted her right arm and dropped it back with a frightened whimper. Someone close to her was coughing, a hard racking cough which tortured her taut nerves. Why? She had no idea where she was. With an effort she opened her eyes and stared at the ceiling. Never had a ceiling appeared to be so far away and never had there been one so grimy, cracked and peeling. She kept staring at it in fascination.

Then the moaning came and she knew it was from her left. With an effort she turned her head and saw that there was a bed next to her. She couldn't begin to understand it. And someone very old and in pain twisted beneath the thin coverlet of this adjoining bed. What did it mean? What kind of a place was this and how had she arrived here?

Panic was quickly replacing her first feelings of dull fascination. Things were happening too rapidly for her to keep track. The racking coughing came again and this was from the right of her bed. She turned that way and saw another bed that contained a pathetic-looking, frail girl propped up by several pillows in a sitting position. The girl held a cloth to her mouth, and as she finished coughing it was stained with blood.

Madeline let a cry of horror escape from her lips. She felt she was a victim of a hideous nightmare and she wanted to escape.

The girl quickly folded the cloth to hide the blood and gazed at her in hollow-eyed wonder. "You've come awake at last!" she said in a weak voice.

Madeline with effort raised herself on an elbow and stared at the emaciated young woman's meek face flanked by stringy red hair.

"Who are you?" she asked the girl, in a hoarse voice quite unlike her own.

"I'm Sarah," the girl replied promptly.

"Sarah?" she was still dazed by it all.

The emaciated girl nodded. "Yes. You was here long before me. When I first came they all said you was going to die. But you didn't."

"No, I didn't," she echoed the girl as she tried to collect her thoughts. She now stared beyond the adjoining bed and saw that she was in a huge room in which beds stretched the entire length and there was another row of beds along the opposite wall. She turned to Sarah again. "Where are we?"

The girl's sunken eyes widened. "Don't you know?"

"If I did I wouldn't ask you," she replied in that same odd, husky voice which was so foreign to her.

"It's the Charity Ward of Boston Hospital," Sarah said. "This is my fourth time here and they say it will be my last. I haven't the strength to sit up anymore. My ma says the consumption has me. I won't get out again."

She listened to the young girl's words with a new sensation of horror. "How would I get to be in the charity ward?" she asked.

"I guess because you was ill and like all the rest of us you couldn't pay," the girl said quite casually. "That's old Nanny Perrin on the other side of you. She's real bad and is soon to die, too."

Madeline gave a frightened glance at the old woman. She had stopped her moaning and twisting about and lay there looking like a corpse, bony hands grasping the coverlet, hollow eyes on the ceiling and sunken mouth agape.

"What time of day is it?" she asked the girl named Sarah.

"Late afternoon, Miss."

She stared around her dully and saw there were windows

63

high in the walls and that a kind of gray light was coming in from outside. She tried to think where she had been last. That was important. If she could remember, she would be able to find out how she had reached this Dante's Inferno of a hospital ward. It was the most frightening place she'd ever seen.

As awareness came gradually to her, she was conscious of the whining of sick voices from the other beds and the moans and choking and coughing which filled the place. The air was fetid with the odor of some nauseating disinfectant. She had an overwhelming desire to get out of bed and flee but she couldn't. She was too weak.

"The doctor was here to see you," Sarah told her. "He has come by every day."

"Oh?" She couldn't think of anything more intelligent to say. She was clenching her hands and trying to think who she was and how she had reached this place. She had a vague remembrance of being somewhere different from this hospital ward, somewhere warm and quiet. Then there had been panic as something dreadful had happened to her. With this memory there was associated pain and cold. Pain and cold.

"What is your name?" the emaciated young girl wanted to know.

She glanced at the girl's meek, wasted face and felt sorry for her. At the same time she attempted to recall her own name. Failing, she was forced to admit, "I don't know."

"You're beautiful," Sarah said. "Even considering what has happened to your nose."

She reached up and touched her nose and found it strangely numb. With a feeling of panic, she asked the girl, "What about my nose?"

"When they found you it was all bashed in," Sarah said. "But they have fixed it up pretty good."

Tears blurred her eyes. It was too much! Finding herself in

a bed in this charity ward was bad enough and now to learn that she'd been disfigured was even worse. She tried to seek out the contours of her nose by running her fingers over it. But the injured part had little or no feeling. Now she understood why her breathing was difficult. No doubt the inner passages had been crushed. She had an urgent desire to look at herself in a mirror.

She turned to the girl. "Do you have a mirror?"

"A tiny one," Sarah said. "I keep it to do my hair. I can't take it to you. I have it here on my table. Can you reach?"

"Yes, I think so," she said eagerly. And she leaned across the bed and stretched out her hand. Sarah had found the mirror and was holding it out in her frail hand. By straining Madeline was able to take hold of it. "Thank you," she told the girl in her new, hoarse voice.

"It's not a good mirror," Sarah said.

She held it in her hands and for a matter of seconds could not bring herself to look in it. Despite her desperate eagerness to get the mirror she was now afraid to use it. At last she very slowly raised it and forced herself to gaze into the murky, oblong glass. What she saw filled her with dismay.

The features were ones she recognized—except the nose! It was flattened and broadened so that it changed her entire expression. She knew this was her own face and yet she looked like a stranger.

"See!" Sarah called from her bed. "I told you it wasn't bad. You're still a beauty!"

She put the mirror down. "A damaged beauty," she said grimly.

At this time two things happened. The dying old woman next to her began to moan again and a middle-aged nurse paddled down the ward in a businesslike manner.

The nurse halted before Madeline's bed and showed surprise on her red, beefy face. "Well, what do you know? You've finally come to!"

"Yes, I have," she said.

"Dr. Harris will be wanting to know that," the nurse said. "I'll leave word for him and he'll be by to see you. Thank goodness now you'll be able to feed yourself."

"How long have I been here?" she asked dully.

"A bit more than a month," the nurse said. "You're in fine shape now compared to then. No one had any idea you'd live."

"What is my name?" Madeline asked.

The nurse looked at her hesitantly. "That's something you will have to take up with Dr. Harris." And she then went on to fuss over Nanny Perrin for a few minutes and somehow managed to quiet the old woman down.

When the nurse moved on, Madeline leaned out and returned the small mirror to the consumptive girl in the bed beside her. "Thank you," she said.

Sarah took her mirror and studied herself in it. "I look a sight," she said with a sigh. "I wasn't so bad looking. But my sickness has made me thin and ugly."

"You're not ugly," Madeline was quick to tell the girl. "And I'm glad to have you as my friend."

Sarah's emaciated face brightened and then quickly shadowed as she was overcome by a sudden spasm of coughing. Madeline turned away to avoid embarrassing the unfortunate girl. She closed her eyes and tried to remember who she was.

The doctor arrived about an hour later. He was youngish and balding. He looked overworked and there was a continual frown on his ordinary, freckled face.

He stood beside her bed and said, "I'm pleased to see you are out of your coma."

"Yes," she said.

"How do you feel?"

"My head aches. My voice is strangely hoarse and I have no memory of how I came here or who I am."

Dr. Harris stood frowning. He thrust his hands in the pocket of his not-quite-clean smock and said, "It's natural for your head to ache. That will pass."

"And my voice?"

He cleared his throat. "I attended you when you first came in. May I say you were a sorry sight. There was damage to your throat in the area of the larynx and your nose was battered in. We were fortunately able to shape your nose into a semblance of itself and it has turned out extremely well. Now that it is healed, it isn't bad at all."

"I had a perfect nose," she said, near tears again.

"You haven't now," Dr. Harris said calmly. "But it is better than most people's, mine included. You notice I have a snub nose."

She gazed up at his serious, plain face and at once felt ashamed of being sorry for herself. It was sinful with others dying all around her. She said, "I didn't mean to sound vain, Doctor."

"What you said was understandable and forgivable," he said with a sudden warmth he hadn't shown before.

"I realize there are many people here worse off than I."

"Be sure of it," the young doctor said, in a return to his brusque manner.

"Where was I found?"

"In an alley on Boylston Street near the Public Gardens. It was the night of a bad snowstorm and it was only a miracle you were discovered before you froze to death. A shoemaker who had his shop in the alley happened to return home late and he stumbled over you in the snow."

She nodded. "I remember the cold and the pain!"

"He had the police come and they brought you here. I was

on late duty that night. You were clad only in a thin night-gown. Your face was a bloodied mess. Someone had pounded it until it was almost a pulp. And as I mentioned before, your throat showed damage."

"I have vague memories of being terrified," she said, "but I can't say by what."

Dr. Harris looked a little more stern than before. "There are girls who ply a trade which places them in danger. We often find one of them in the streets badly battered. My first thought was that you were a member of that unfortunate sorority. But now I begin to doubt it."

She blushed and protested, "I don't know who I am, but I'm certain I wasn't a woman of the streets."

"I can tell that now," he said. "You talk like a lady."

"My voice is so hoarse and strange," she said.

"Be patient. I'm sure the hoarseness will eventually go. It could take months or perhaps a year. There was damage done and it will take nature time to repair it."

"Who would do such terrible things to me?"

"I can't imagine," the doctor said.

"I was left there to die."

"I would say so. No one could have lived long in that cold. And you were badly injured."

"Someone attacked me and then left me there to die," she repeated.

"Took you there to die," Dr. Harris corrected her. "You quite clearly were not strolling down Boylston Street in a nightgown in a snowstorm in the middle of the night. You were attacked somewhere else and then taken there. Probably in a sleigh."

"I remember that I was warm and it was a very quiet place," she said, straining to recall it all.

"Probably your home, wherever that happens to be," Dr.

Harris said. "The police have made inquiries, but with no identification it is not going to be easy to find out who you are. It is likely that within a few days your own memory will come back again and you'll be able to fill in all the answers yourself."

"Oh, I hope so!" she said.

"For the time being rest and try and make more progress," he said.

"I find it very depressing here," she told him.

"So do I," he said dryly. "I'm afraid hospitals are inclined to be like that. And we have no private rooms for charity cases."

Again she felt embarrassed. She said, "Dr. Harris, I am grateful for all that you've done for me. But finding myself here like this has been a dreadful shock."

"Naturally."

"If I only knew who I am."

He said, "I keep thinking I may have met you somewhere before. And yet the face eludes me."

"Not much wonder," she said bitterly, "the new configuration of my nose makes me look quite different."

"You remember what you looked like?"

"Yes."

"That's good," he said. "I wonder that your friends, or your family, possibly your husband, haven't reported you missing to the police."

A feeling of fear crept through her. "Perhaps I have no friends or family."

"Almost everyone has."

"I can be certain of one thing," she said grimly.

"What is that?"

"I have a mortal enemy."

Dr. Harris nodded uneasily. "Yes. I suppose we must agree to that."

"An enemy who probably thinks me safely dead."

"Probably," the young doctor said. "I don't believe there was more than a brief paragraph in the newspaper about you. And I'm doubtful if the mention was in all the papers."

"I wonder who it was and where he or she is now," she said.

"If your memory returns you'll likely have the answers to all those questions," Dr. Harris said.

He left her and then dinner was served. On this evening it happened to be a thick meat and vegetable soup. While it was served rather roughly from a large pot carried from bed to bed, the food tasted excellent. After the meal and a strong cup of tea she felt much better.

Almost at once she fell into a deep exhausted sleep and did not wake until morning. The first thing she noticed when she awoke was that Nanny Perrin had gone and there was a grim-faced, elderly stout woman in her bed.

Sarah supplied the information concerning the vanished Nanny. "Went in the night, she did," Sarah observed dolefully. "They came and wheeled her out before dawn."

"The poor woman is better out of her misery," Madeline said.

"The Lord's will," the emaciated Sarah said piously.

On the second day of being fully conscious of her surroundings, Madeline began to adjust to them. The stout woman on her left was a victim of Bright's disease and not talkative. Madeline was grateful for that as Sarah kept up a steady conversation with her. She could tell the dying girl was lonesome and so didn't mind giving her attention.

She still racked her brain to remember her past and what had happened the night she'd been left in the snow to die. And she still had no success. Dr. Harris came to pay his regular call and seemed pleased with her condition. She asked to get up but he refused permission for a few days longer.

It was on the afternoon of the fourth day that the unexpected happened. She was sitting up in bed talking with Sarah when she noticed a nurse coming down the corridor followed by a short stout man. She paid no particular attention to them until the nurse paused at her bed to say, "You have a visitor."

The man came to her bedside and the moment she saw his face she recognized him. "Sam Elder!" she exclaimed.

The theatre manager's face was filled with emotion. "I have found you at last!" he declared.

"I've been here without memory," she told him. And as she stared at him it all began to come back.

"Madeline! What have they done to you?" he lamented.

"They haven't improved on me," she told him wryly. And now she knew. She was Madeline Renais and she had starred in his theatre. Then Raymond Copeland had taken her to live in that grim old house in Brookline.

Sam turned to the nurse. "I must get this young woman out of here. She must have a private room! Who will I see?"

The nurse looked uneasy. "Dr. Harris, I suppose," she said.

"Very well, take me to him at once," Sam said with all his usual authority. And he told Madeline, "I'll be back just as soon as I can."

"It's all right," she told him.

But he was already on his way out with the nurse, talking at his usual rapid pace. She supposed that he was telling the woman who she was.

Sarah spoke to her, "Was that your gentleman friend come to take you away?" Her tone was forlorn.

"He is a friend," she explained. "And he probably will take me out of here."

Sarah's thin face took on a wistful expression. "I shall miss you."

She was touched. "And I shall miss you. But they'll likely put someone else in here whom you can talk to."

The girl in the other bed sighed. "No one as nice as you. I know that."

Madeline said, "If I do leave I promise I'll come back to see you."

Sarah's face lit up. "Will you, honestly?"

"I promise."

The dying girl sighed. "At least I shall have that to look forward to."

Madeline talked to Sarah and tried to comfort her. At the same time her mind was miles away on her own affairs. Her memory was coming back with a vengeance. Just the sight of Sam's familiar face had been the key to her returning memory, and she was able to recall everything up to and including the night of the attack on her.

Sam Elder came back into the ward with Dr. Harris and the nurse. Now he was giving Dr. Harris a lecture and she was sure that it would bring results of some sort. The party of three came to her bed again and Dr. Harris stepped close to her.

The young doctor said, "Mr. Elder tells me we are entertaining a very famous person. I knew I should have recognized you, Miss Renais. I saw your revue several times."

"Thank you," she said.

"You were excellent in it," Dr. Harris went on. "Mr. Elder is arranging to have you transferred to a private room at once. You will remain there for a few days until we're sure you are well enough to leave."

"That is very kind of Mr. Elder," she said.

Sam beamed at her from the foot of the bed. "We'll have you in a nice private room in a half-hour."

As usual he was as good as his word. Within the hour, she found herself enjoying the luxury of a large, private room. Once Sam had her safely installed, he crossed to the window, opened it and drawing out his cigar case, selected one of his long black cigars.

Carefully biting the end off, he proceeded to light it and take a long, satisfying puff. He came to her bedside and said, "Forgive me, but I was starved for a cigar. They wouldn't let me smoke out there."

She smiled. "They needn't know what happens in here."

"Exactly," Sam said, and then he began to pace back and forth. "You must be wondering how I came to find you?"

"Yes."

His ugly, squarish face showed annoyance. "I would have been looking for you weeks earlier but for the stupidity of my theatre janitor. The morning after the police found you battered in the snow, a number of trunks containing your belongings were delivered to the theatre by some unknown driver. They were labeled with your name and the janitor stored them away without telling me."

"So you knew nothing about them?"

"Nothing," Sam said, pausing with his cigar in hand. "Then a few days ago some other things arrived and my stage manager noticed the trunks and wondered about them. He came and told me. I examined them and found they'd been hastily packed and sent to me."

"What did you do then?"

"I called at the Copeland Bank and asked for Raymond."

"And?"

Sam Elder showed disgust. "I was informed he was out of the city. So I asked to speak to his father."

"I can imagine Thomas Copeland gave you a cold reception," she said.

73

"Cold is hardly the word for it. Icy would be much better. I told him about the luggage and asked where you were. I had an idea you and Raymond might have been quietly married and that you'd gone off on a honeymoon together. Though I still wasn't able to understand about the trunks with your clothing."

"What did Raymond's father say?"

"He treated me as if I were a pauper asking for a loan," Sam complained. "He said that you and Raymond had some sort of quarrel and that you left the house without a word to anyone during a crisis when his elderly mother was very ill."

"Go on," she urged him grimly.

"He said they had waited for a day or two, expecting to hear from you or have you come back. But you didn't return. He felt you might have need of your things and so sent them to me at the theatre, expecting I would know where you were."

"What about Raymond?"

"He claimed that his son had been feeling unwell and so he'd sent Raymond to a warmer climate for a few months. He is still away."

"And then?"

"Then I contacted the police. And they remembered that on the night of your supposed leaving the Copelands in a rage, a girl was found in an alley on Boylston Street. They said she'd been badly beaten and was in a coma. They weren't even sure she was alive, but they did tell me this girl was at Boston City Hospital."

"And so you came and found me."

"Yes."

She lay back against the several pillows which had been arranged to make her sitting up more comfortable. "So now we have the whole story."

"Not by any means," Sam said angrily. "Someone at the Copeland house did this to you and they should be made to pay. You must turn all the information over to the police. Accuse the Copelands."

She shook her head wearily. "Don't you see? It wouldn't do any good. Thomas Copeland would stick to his story that I left on my own. What happened to me after that would not be his responsibility. I might have been attacked anywhere by strangers unknown to him."

"Would that story be accepted?"

"Of course. The Copelands are one of Boston's first families."

Sam took an angry puff on his cigar and came to her bedside to ask, "What really did happen?"

She sighed. "It's true that Raymond and I weren't getting on all that well. And he mentioned that he was feeling ill and went up to bed early. I chatted with his father a few minutes and thought he was behaving strangely. He was very cold towards me. I then went to my room. I awoke in the middle of the night with a feeling of terror. I was sure there was someone in the room with me."

"And?"

"Within a few seconds I saw a figure emerge out of the shadows."

"Who?"

"I don't know. Someone in a black hood with eye slits and a black robe. I screamed and then the assailant seized me by the throat. All my memories after that are of confusion, pain and cold."

Sam's ugly face was wrathful. "So it was one of them."

"I'm almost positive it was Thomas Copeland. He behaved in a very strange way that night. He had tried to buy me off from marrying Raymond."

"Then we must find a way to prove Thomas Copeland the guilty one," the theatre manager said.

"It won't be as easy to do as it is in one of your plays," she warned him.

Sam studied her with distress. "They must pay. Look what they've done to you!"

"You haven't congratulated me on my new nose," she said.

"It changes your looks. I'd hardly recognize you!"

"My theatre career is finished," she said.

"You don't look bad," Sam hastened to say. Then he added limply, "But different from before."

"I have seen myself in a mirror," she said. "I won't win any more beauty prizes. But worst of all is my voice."

"You're very hoarse."

"Dr. Harris says that the condition can only be cured by time. Nature is sometimes a slow healer. He claims it may require months or even a year or two before I regain my normal voice."

"But you will regain it?"

"He hopes so."

Sam took another puff on his cigar. "It's one of the worst things I've ever heard of. It wasn't bad enough for Raymond to take you out of the theatre, he's let this happen to you."

"Don't blame him," she said. "He had a bad headache that night. His father made up the story of my leaving and he believed it. And then to make sure he didn't try to find me, his father sent him away for a holiday."

Sam Elder nodded. "It all fits in," he agreed. "I'd say that Thomas Copeland attacked you and then somehow got your body into a sleigh and dumped you in that alley."

"Not a very pretty story."

"Vile," the theatre manager fumed.

"I'm too weak to care much at the moment," she said. "I would like to know when Raymond is returning. Do you think you might be able to find out?"

"I'll try," the squat man said.

"And can you bring some of my clothes here to me? I have nothing to leave in."

"It will be taken care of at once," he promised.

"I need to get out of here," she said. "I'll not mend properly until I'm on the outside."

"I agree," Sam said. "I'll work on it."

"Until you came into the hospital my memory was a blank. Now things are rushing back into my mind!"

"At least you suffered no mental injury," he said.

"I think not. How can one be sure, yet?" she asked.

"You seem remarkably alert now that you have your memory," he said.

She gave him a knowing look. "My mind may be as scarred as my face."

Sam showed embarrassment. "You mustn't worry about your face. You look different, but you're still attractive. If I could be sure your voice would return I'd start making plans for a new show."

"Too early for that yet."

"We will do another show. I'm positive of it."

She studied him with adoring eyes. "You've always been such a staunch friend, Sam."

He knocked the ash from his cigar and shrugged. "I haven't so many friends that I can ignore them."

"Even if I fully recover you mustn't count on my returning to the theatre."

"Why not?"

"I'm still engaged to Raymond."

Sam's eyebrows raised. "You'd have anything to do with

the Copelands after this?"

"I can't blame him."

"He didn't try to find you."

"Because he believed what his father told him and he's very proud. He'd wait for me to get in touch with him. Then they sent him away to make certain that he didn't relent and make some attempt to locate me."

The squat man sighed. "You go out of your way to make him seem lily white."

"In this instance I'm sure that he is."

"You blame Thomas Copeland."

"I think he's the one, but who knows? He may only have been in on it. Any of the others could have attacked me. James hated me and so did his wife Alice."

Sam looked shocked. "You're saying a woman might have beaten you up that way?"

"Alice could have. She's large and very strong. And then there's Juliet. She's athletic for a girl and she had been jealous of me from the moment I arrived in Brookline."

"So it could have been any one of them?" Sam said with a frustrated note in his harsh voice.

She nodded slowly. "Or all of them working together. They wanted to eliminate me and they managed very well."

Sam said, "They'll find out now that they failed."

"No," she said. "I don't want that. Not yet. You mustn't tell anyone. For the time being I want to remain dead."

CHAPTER FIVE

And dead Madeline remained as far as the rest of Boston was concerned. Sam rented a cottage for her in the outskirts of the city in his sister's name. And on the day she left the hospital, Sam took her there in his own carriage. It was mid-March and the end of a mild winter. There was no snow on the ground and the air was beginning to warm with the promise of an early spring.

Before Madeline left the hospital she went to visit the dying Sarah in her ward bed. She was alarmed to find the girl greatly weakened, and the nurse told her she had hemorrhaged during the night, indicating the end could be near.

Madeline bent close to her and saw that her eyes were bright with fever. She said, "I've come back as I promised."

"I knew you would," Sarah whispered with a pathetic smile.

"I'd like to do something for you before I leave," she said.

"Nothing now," the girl said in the same whisper. "You were kind to me when it mattered. Now I just want to rest and go to sleep."

Madeline's eyes brimmed with tears. "What if I have you put in a private room? Would you like that?"

"No," the girl said. "I don't want to die alone."

"Nonsense," she said. "I'll be back to visit you many times again!"

"Yes," Sarah whispered with another faint smile. "Yes." And she closed her eyes.

On the way out of the hospital, Madeline talked with Dr.

Harris. "What about Sarah?" she asked.

The young doctor looked gloomy. "Done for! I shouldn't be surprised if she dies before the day is over. I've told her mother."

"It's that bad?"

"I'm afraid so," he said. "Since she returned this last time there has been no hope."

"I became very fond of her."

The balding, young doctor nodded with a friendly look on his plain face. "I know. She told me. Remarkable how she talks with me. I know most of her secrets."

"You've been more than kind to her!"

"And so have you," he said. "But there's nothing else you can do. You mustn't grieve over her. You need all your strength to regain your own health."

"That I'm alive I have mostly to thank you," she said.

"I'm glad I was able to help," Dr. Harris told her. He extended his hand to her. "Best of luck, Miss Renais. I hope you regain your voice and that you are able to return to the stage."

"Thank you," she said with a smile. "If I do, I'll send you tickets for you and your wife."

He smiled now. "You can send the tickets but I'll have to find someone to take. My life here hasn't allowed me time for a wife thus far."

"I'm not surprised," she said, studying the plain young man with sympathy. "But you mustn't forget to live your own life in your dedication to others."

And so they parted on this note. She was surprised that she had become so fond of this quiet, humble and talented young man. Yet it was not so strange; he had saved her life.

The cottage which Sam Elder had rented for her was small but pleasant, with a nice garden in the rear. He also engaged a housekeeper-companion, a Mrs. Ennis, who had worked in his theatre as a wardrobe mistress. As soon as she was installed in the cottage, Madeline insisted on writing checks to repay the theatre manager. She had an adequate bank account and could afford to pay for her convalescence.

As the days grew longer and warmer she spent more time outside. She and Mrs. Ennis planned what they would do with the garden. Sam drove out from the city at least twice a week and usually brought her news of the theatre and other Boston happenings.

On one of the afternoons when he visited her, he sank down in an easy chair in the parlor and said, "I have some definite word about Raymond Copeland at last."

She was standing in the center of the room and was at once eager to hear the news. For some weeks they'd tried to learn of her fiancé's whereabouts without any success.

"What have you found out?" she asked.

"He has been in the south of France," Sam said, lighting one of his big black cigars. "He's expected home in another week."

"At last!" she said.

"Are you going to let him know you're here?" Sam asked.

A shadow crossed her face. "I haven't decided."

He said, "I understand the family is moving to their island place in another month. They just come up to the bank once or twice a week during the summer."

"I remember Martha Copeland speaking to me about the house on the island. What is the name of it?"

Sam sat back in the easy chair and puffed on his cigar. He said, "The name of their island house is Pinecrest, in the town of Dark Harbor on a little island off Cape Cod called Pirate Island."

"Yes," she agreed. "I remember all those names now."

"Dark Harbor has a big colony of wealthy Bostonians, headed by your good friend Thomas Copeland," Sam said with a note of sarcasm.

"I'm not surprised," she said. "How have you come by all this information?"

"Hudson Strout is my lawyer. You remember him."

"Of course," she said. "I suppose he is still engaged to Juliet?"

"They still see each other but he has not pressed her to name a date for their wedding," Sam said with relish. "I have an idea he'd like to get out of it."

"He's much too nice for her!"

"I agree," the theatre manager said. "But the fact he goes there fairly often has benefits. I get my information from him. He says the old woman, Martha, has made a good recovery and is going to Dark Harbor. At the moment the family is seeking a good companion-nurse for her."

"That should be an easy job," she said. "Martha is the nicest of the Copelands if you exclude Raymond."

Sam hunched in his chair. "Before you say too much about Raymond let me give you some news."

She had a sudden apprehension that what Sam had to tell her might not be pleasant. She said, "Go on."

"Raymond is bringing a girl back with him. A British girl he met in Cannes named Ann Gresham. He's asked her to marry him. I hate to be the one to tell you this."

His words had a painful effect on her. She sought out the nearest chair and sank into it. She felt that she might faint.

Staring at him anxiously, she said, "Are you sure?"

"Yes."

She sat nervously twisting her hands. "How could he?"

"He thinks you have coldly deserted him," the theatre manager reminded her.

"But he should have sought me out and asked me before doing anything like this!"

"You said he was proud."

"Yes."

"So he accepted what his people told him about you. However, the joke is on them. They rid themselves of you only to be caught up in a worse situation. Miss Gresham is churchmouse poor and was working at one of the hotels as a dancing girl. You can guess how the Copelands feel about her!"

"At least Raymond stays with theatrical types," she said grimly, the first of the shock over.

"They're already in an uproar and planning to break up the marriage, from what Hudson Strout tells me."

Madeline gave him a bleak look. "I hope they won't be as cruel in doing it as they were with me."

"I hope not."

"When I came to in the hospital all my rings were gone."

Sam Elder laughed. "Rings come cheap for the Copelands. I suspect he's given one to this new girl. He's likely so infatuated with Ann Gresham he's forgotten about you completely."

She stared at him. "You really believe he's that much in love with her?"

"Why should you care?" Sam wanted to know.

"I'm afraid I still do," she said. "I think we would have been happy enough if it hadn't been for his family."

"What about Raymond himself? He was still as wild as ever after he became engaged to you and he drank to the point where it was detrimental to his health."

Madeline's attractive face was grim. "I think family pressure could also account for that."

"You want to believe in him."

"Perhaps," she said. "I know he was not to blame for what happened to me. And I only fear for this girl. Who can tell what cruelty they may inflict on her?"

Sam Elder shrugged. "There's nothing you can do about it. I say you are well out of it."

"I wish I hadn't found all this out," she worried.

"Perhaps I oughtn't to have told you," the theatre manager said. "But you asked me to keep you informed."

"And you were right to do so," she agreed.

Sam frowned. "You know I have never told Hudson Strout about you. And I think I should. He might be able to keep an eye on this girl and help her."

"You mean if he knew what the Copelands did to me?"

"Yes."

She debated a moment. "Do you think you can trust him to keep the information to himself?"

"I consider him a most reliable person," Sam said. "He has done well for me as my lawyer."

Madeline felt inclined to agree with Sam. It was terribly important that her secret be kept but she also saw that Hudson Strout might be able to protect this Ann Gresham from a similar fate if he was able to warn her.

She said, "I don't want the Copelands to know that I'm alive and have recovered. I'm sure they think I died in that alley."

"You only escaped death by a miracle," Sam Elder said.

"Yet I would like to let Hudson Strout know that at least one of them tried to kill me."

"I leave it up to you," the squat man said, rising from his chair. "It is time I drove back to the city."

She said, "The theatre is closed Sunday night. Why don't you bring Hudson Strout out here to dinner. In the meanwhile you can tell him about me."

Sam's ugly face showed relief. "An excellent idea! And I'm glad you've decided to tell him. I was hoping you would."

"There is always a risk."

"Not in confiding in him," Sam assured her as they walked towards the front door of the cottage. "I'm not willing to stand behind many people but I am behind him."

She offered him a small smile. "That is a strong argument in his favor. I've not seen you make many wrong judgments about people."

Sam gave her a meaningful look. "And for the record I've never liked Raymond Copeland, despite your feelings for him. And I think his turning to this other girl so soon proves something."

"Let's not discuss it anymore just now," she said.

"I'm sorry," Sam said. "I'll see you on Sunday at seven and bring Hudson Strout along."

After Sam Elder left she spent a long while sitting in a chair by a window overlooking the garden. She stared out at the emerging green of the new growth and thought about all she had heard. It had come as a shock to her and she realized that she had gone on hoping that she and Raymond would one day be reconciled despite what had happened.

She had been staying in the background until she heard of his return. Then she had planned to confront him and tell him the truth—that she hadn't deserted him as he'd been told. But all that was changed now. Raymond had quickly shown an interest in someone new. Could she blame him? Perhaps not. His hurt pride probably had sent him along the path of this new romance.

What was left for her to do? Should she simply forget the Copelands and what they had done to her or should she still try to contact Raymond? Sam's idea of letting Hudson Strout know what had happened was the best way.

Madeline still had sufficient funds to live in comfort for a while. She debated returning to Paris. This again seemed appealing, but she could not resume her career. Her voice was still hoarse, which would not do for the stage. And she was self-conscious about her appearance although her housekeeper daily assured her that she was still a beauty.

It would take more time, she decided with a sigh. And she tried to put the whole business out of her mind and concentrate on working in her garden.

But the news about Raymond and his new fiancé had upset her far more than she'd been willing to admit. That night she had frightening nightmares in which she was back in the old mansion in Brookline being threatened. She dreamt the entire episode of the attacker in the black hood and robe coming into her room and seizing her by the throat.

She awoke screaming! And when Mrs. Ennis came running into the room in her nightrobe she had to hastily apologize for causing such an uproar. Later when she was alone in the darkness of the room she stared up into the shadows and realized that the information Sam Elder had brought her had taken a great toll.

It was not until the next afternoon that a plan suddenly formed in her mind. She was standing before the dresser mirror in her bedroom studying herself and thinking how much her appearance had been altered by the new structure of her nose. And then it came to her!

Impulsively she sat down and taking a pair of tweezers she began to pluck at her eyebrows and alter their shape. Next she tried doing her long, raven-black hair in different ways. None of the styles suited her. She got up and called Mrs. Ennis into the room.

The former wardrobe mistress joined her and at once said, "What have you done to your eyebrows, Miss Renais?

You've changed your expression!"

She smiled. "Do you like it?"

"No," the stout woman said frankly. "I don't think so."

"That's too bad," she said. "Because I'm going to make some other changes and I need your help."

"Other changes?" Mrs. Ennis looked concerned.

"Yes," she said. "My hair is too long. I want it clipped to at least half its present length."

The housekeeper gasped. "Oh, no, Miss! You've always worn your hair long and in an up-do. It has been most becoming. I can't imagine you without that pompadour!"

"I intend to change the style and wear it drawn straight back."

"Straight back! You'll look like a little country girl," Mrs. Ennis lamented.

"Get the scissors," Madeline said as she stood there with her lovely flowing hair reaching well past her shoulders.

"Miss!" the housekeeper stood firm in protest.

"I mean it. If you won't help cut my hair I'm going to do it myself."

"It's all wrong!"

"And my decision. I'll not do nearly as good a job as you," she warned the woman. "So what do you say?"

"You don't leave me any choice," Mrs. Ennis said unhappily.

After some more argument between them, the housekeeper went to get the scissors. When she returned Madeline sat before the dresser mirror and directed her in the cutting of her hair. She watched and gave careful instructions. And she was callous in the shearing of the lovely, long hair. By the time the operation was completed, her hair was shoulder-length and the floor around her was covered with shorn tresses.

Mrs. Ennis stood back emotionally, the scissors still in hand. "It's a terrible thing you made me do, Miss."

Madeline smiled and taking the remaining hair in her hands she drew it back from her forehead tightly and tied it in a ponytail.

"There," she said. "That's exactly what I want!"

Mrs. Ennis studied her sadly. "It doesn't look like Madeline Renais."

She glanced at her. "Who says I want to look like Madeline Renais?"

"I don't understand," the former wardrobe mistress said.

Madeline got up and went over to the woman. "You're adept at helping with makeup. I remember that from the theatre days."

"What has that to do with anything?"

"I want to dye my hair," she told her. "I have decided I want to be a blonde."

"You a blonde?"

"Why not? I'm sure you know the ingredients I need for a proper dye job. I want you to go to the nearest pharmacy and buy those items for me, and then you can help me go to work on my hair."

Mrs. Ennis seemed to be on the brink of tears. "It's simply a sacrilege," she protested.

Madeline smiled at her. "Maybe so, but let us see how it looks, shall we? And one other thing, I want you to visit an optical shop and buy me a pair of frames with plain glass in them. The kind we used on the stage when someone wore glasses who didn't require them."

"It doesn't make any sense!" Mrs. Ennis said with despair.

"Don't worry about that," Madeline told her. "Just do as I say."

With much lamentation the housekeeper finally set out on

the errands and Madeline eagerly awaited her return. She had set her mind on a course and she was determined to follow it through.

The next day she worked in the garden in the morning and in the afternoon she and Mrs. Ennis spent several hours bleaching her hair. By the time they finished, she was a striking blonde. The transformation was amazing and she found herself thoroughly satisfied despite Mrs. Ennis' laments.

When her hair was properly dry, she combed it and arranged it in the severe ponytail which she'd tested earlier. After that she put on the prim spectacles. Even they did a lot to contribute to the effect. This done she marched out to the kitchen and presented herself to the former wardrobe mistress.

Mrs. Ennis shook her head and said, "I declare I wouldn't know you. You look like another person."

She smiled broadly. "That is what I plan to be, another person."

And as if to prove this she continued for the balance of the week wearing her hair in this fashion and always donning the glasses. She found suitable dresses in her wardrobe to alter and make more plain, and she wore a different one every day.

Thus, it was, when Sunday arrived that she answered the door when Sam Elder rang the bell to announce he and Hudson Strout. She opened the door demurely and stood staring at them as if they were strangers.

Hat in hand the squat, mustached Sam registered uneasiness as he said in his harsh voice, "We've come to see Miss Renais. Is she in?"

She nodded and stood back for them to enter. Sam Elder seemed much surprised. He was wearing his best black suit and Hudson Strout was wearing a dark green outfit which showed fine tailoring.

She silently led them into her neat, little parlor and motioned them to be seated. The two men exchanged puzzled glances and then sat on the sofa together. They were plainly waiting for Madeline to present herself.

Standing in the middle of the room facing them, she said, "I don't suppose you know who I am?" She didn't attempt to disguise the hoarse voice she'd been plagued with since the night of the attack.

Sam Elder stared at her for a long moment, then he gaped and jumped up. "Madeline!" he cried. "What the devil are you doing?"

She laughed. "I was sure you'd recognize me when I spoke. Voices can betray one almost quicker than anything else."

Now the good-looking Hudson Strout joined Sam in standing. He eyed her incredulously and said, "I didn't even recognize the voice."

"Because you haven't heard her speak since that monstrous assault when her larynx was injured," Sam Elder said. And he came over and placed an arm fondly around her. "You surely played a trick on us, but what have you done to yourself?"

"Not too much," she said. "Let us all relax while I serve some sherry."

Not until they were all seated with their sherry glasses full did she begin to talk about what she had done and the purpose of it.

"I wanted to see if I could deceive Sam," she said. "He knows me better than most people."

"I didn't recognize you at all," the theatre manager said taking a puff on the cigar he'd just lighted.

"Then maybe I'll have the courage I'll require to pursue a

plan I have in mind," she said.

"What sort of plan?" Sam wanted to know.

She took a sip of her sherry and turned to Hudson Strout. "Sam has filled you in on all that happened to me?"

"Yes," the young lawyer said. "And may I offer you my deep sympathy and say that I think it was the most dastardly thing I have ever heard of. I didn't think the Copelands capable of such primitive cruelty."

"Neither did I," she said with a bleak smile. "Otherwise I wouldn't have remained in that house."

"Sam hinted that you believe Thomas Copeland was the one who actually attacked you and left you out in the snow to die," the young man said.

"I think it had to be him," she said. "The only two people in the family I can eliminate on account of illness are Martha Copeland and Raymond. Any of the others are suspect but I feel most strongly that it was Raymond's father."

Hudson Strout said cynically, "That respected leader of Boston's banking profession."

"I could tell you a lot about some of our so-called Boston Brahmins," Sam Elder said studying his cigar. "Not any of it fit for Madeline's ears."

The young lawyer said, "But I have known Thomas Copeland for so long. I recognized him as a cold fish and odd. But this goes way beyond that. If it could be proved, you'd have the pleasure of seeing him in prison, Miss Renais."

"But it obviously can't be proved," she said.

"That unfortunately is the case," the young lawyer agreed. "Juliet fed me the story of your leaving the house in a huff. She made it seem that you were merely a temperamental and spoiled actress who didn't care anything about Raymond and selfishly went away on your own."

"And you believed it?" she asked.

Hudson Strout looked embarrassed. "Let us say I didn't think it sounded like you. Yet in the face of the evidence and the story they all offered I had little choice but to believe them."

Solemnly, she said, "And so did everyone else."

"They perpetrated a near-perfect crime," Sam Elder declared finishing the rest of his sherry and placing the glass on the endtable near him.

"I agree," she said. "And now I plan to have my revenge."

Sam Elder's square face showed worry. "I hope you're not planning anything foolish."

"I hope not," she said.

"What have you in mind?" Hudson Strout asked.

"I want to warn that new girlfriend of Raymond's in some way," she said. "You may be able to help. That is why we have confided in you and why Sam has brought you here today."

"I understand," the young man said.

She asked bluntly, "How much loyalty do you owe Juliet?"

At the mention of Raymond's sister, the young man frowned. He said, "Juliet and I have had a series of quarrels. In the interim she has been dating other men. She is still wearing my ring, and I still see her but the mad romance between us is finished. I've been disenchanted by her coldness, her selfishness and now this new revelation about the Copelands has added to my disgust. I think I can safely say that Juliet and I will never marry."

"I'm glad for your sake," she said.

The young lawyer asked, "What about you and Raymond?"

She blushed. "I think it late to discuss that. He has turned to someone else."

Sam Elder said, "Make no pretense. We both know you're

still in love with him even though he doesn't deserve your love. Tell us what you have in mind."

She said, "You gave me the idea."

"I did?" he said, puzzled.

"Yes. The other day when you said the Copelands were moving to their Dark Harbor house and had been advertising for a woman companion for Raymond's grandmother."

Sam Elder leaned forward in his chair. "They are seeking a companion-nurse for Martha Copeland. So?"

"So I plan to be that nurse," she said.

"You what?" Sam exclaimed.

"I'm going to apply for the job."

Hudson Strout shook his head. "That would be too risky. Your going back there could end in disaster for you. They might see through your disguise and complete the job they attempted last time."

"Never," she said. "I'm prepared this time. And anyway neither of you recognized me."

"True," Sam Elder admitted. "But I think it too risky."

"So do I," Hudson Strout agreed.

"I don't," she said. "In fact I plan to visit the bank tomorrow and apply to Thomas Copeland for the position."

Sam Elder chuckled. "You mean it, don't you?"

"I do," she said.

The young lawyer stared at her. "If you should get the position what do you hope to accomplish?"

"Several things," she said.

"Would you mind telling us what they might be?" Sam asked.

"No," she said. "I want to live with the Copelands again and try to discover which of them attacked me. I also want to protect this Ann Gresham from the same sort of tragedy which befell me. And before I leave, I would like to revenge myself on the guilty party and let Raymond know that I didn't desert him."

"That's a pretty difficult program you've set up for yourself," Hudson Strout warned her.

"I'll not rest until I try it," she said.

Sam Elder looked dubious. "You say revenge yourself on the Copelands. How do you expect to go about that? And how do you think you're going to discover the guilty one? They are ice-cold and not the type to break down and confess."

"Excuse me a moment," she said. "I'll be right back." And, enjoying the puzzled look on their faces, she hurried from the parlor to her bedroom.

There she quickly donned a long, flowing black wig similar to her own hair before she'd cut and bleached it. Then she picked up a black eye-liner and drew in her brows as they had been before she plucked them. After that she took a stick of white grease paint and carefully drew a straight line down the bridge of her nose. Next she touched a darker grease paint to the sides of her nose and powdered it all over. She had earlier removed her glasses and now she surveyed herself in the mirror and was satisfied.

The transformation back to her former appearance accomplished, she returned to the parlor and stood in the doorway facing her two guests. The reaction was immediate and striking.

Sam Elder stood up and in a hushed voice said, "Madeline! It's you again! Your nose looks just as it did! How have you managed it?"

"Remarkable!" Hudson Strout said, also on his feet.

She smiled. "Don't come too close or the illusion will be ruined. But at a distance or in the semi-darkness it is very good, isn't it?"

"Madeline Renais reborn," Sam said with reverence.

"No," she corrected him, "the ghost of Madeline Renais!"

"The ghost?" Sam echoed.

"Yes," she said. "And that is how I plan to get my revenge on the Copelands and perhaps taunt the killer into revealing himself. The ghost of Madeline Renais is going to follow the family to Dark Harbor and haunt them!"

"I like the idea," Sam Elder admitted. "It's theatrical! But then it's risky."

"Not at all," she said. "They won't even recognize my voice. And when I appear as a ghost I shall be silent or whisper. They'll never connect the meek little blonde in glasses with the ghost."

Hudson Strout eyed her approvingly. "You're magnificent! You have thought it all out."

"I know I can manage it," she said. "Perhaps just anyone couldn't. But I'm an actress. I know how to create an illusion and carry it through."

Sam Elder sighed. "I suppose you'll do it no matter what we say?"

"I'm afraid that is so," she agreed with a wan smile.

"In the face of such determination what can one say?" Hudson Strout asked.

Sam Elder nodded. "Since you're bound to go ahead with this, Madeline, let us know how we can help you."

She smiled. "We can discuss that at the excellent dinner Mrs. Ennis has prepared. But first let me get out of this wig and take off my make-up."

Dinner was a success although Sam complained of her change back to the plain girl in the spectacles. He said, "I'd much rather you had entertained us in your make-up. Then you really looked like Madeline Renais."

"I'm afraid the real Madeline Renais did die that night in

the snow," she said in a quiet way. "I feel a different person now. I must go on in my own way. I can't return to what I was. The Copelands saw to that."

"No one can blame you for bitterness," Hudson Strout said. "If you get the position and I'm invited to Dark Harbor you can depend on me for any support I can offer."

She gave the young lawyer a grateful glance. "I felt that I could."

They sat over coffee and discussed every angle of her plan until she felt there were no loopholes. It had to be completely sound and she felt that it was. She saw the two men out and bade them goodnight. It had been an interesting experience and she now had the confidence to go to Boston in the morning to confront Thomas Copeland and ask him for the position as his mother's companion.

The last visit she'd had with Martha Copeland had been just before she was stricken with pneumonia. She'd seemed old and frail then, so by this time she would really need care. The old woman's broken hip added to her problems. But Madeline had no qualms about acting as her companion. If there was a single Copeland she didn't hate, it was poor old Martha. Of course there was also Raymond, who in spite of his faults she still loved, but because of the turn of events this no longer mattered. He was lost to her.

CHAPTER SIX

Madeline awoke to a beautiful, sunny morning and the strong temptation to remain at home and work in her garden. But she knew if she evaded going ahead with her plan now she would never do anything about it. So she got up and, as soon as she had breakfast, sent word to the local livery stable that she wanted a carriage. While Mrs. Ennis was away delivering this message Madeline carefully dressed and made up for the role she was going to play.

By the time the carriage arrived with Mrs. Ennis in it she was ready. She waited until the stout woman came into the house and then told her, "I'll be back as soon as I can. Don't worry about me."

Mrs. Ennis looked upset. "You know I'm bound to worry."

She patted her gently on the arm. "No need." And then she went on her way.

The drive in the open carriage was enjoyable. She used her parasol to protect her against the sun. The city was busy when they reached the financial district where the Copeland Bank was located. She asked the driver to wait as he helped her down.

She found the building with the black and gold sign which boldly announced, "North East Bank, Thomas Copeland and Sons." She stepped inside and was met by an elderly man in a Prince Albert coat.

"Can I be of some service, Miss?"

"Yes," she said, behaving in an awed manner in keeping

with her role of simple country girl.

"Whom do you wish to see?" the old man inquired.

"Your President, Mr. Thomas Copeland," she said. "I have come in answer to his advertisement for a companion for his mother."

The elderly gentleman in the Prince Albert looked worried. "I'm not sure he'd wish to discuss this during business hours. You should have gone to his home."

She pretended innocence. "But Brookline is very distant, and I am new in the city from my home in Portland, Maine. I wouldn't know where to find it."

The side-whiskered major-domo reflected on this. After a moment of rubbing his chin he announced, "I will discuss this with his clerk and return to you."

He marched off importantly leaving her standing alone on the marble floor. At the counters all around her, business was being transacted. There was an almost religious air of decorum about the high-ceilinged and columned room. The customers were all well-dressed males and they stood at the various wickets discussing their transactions in softly-modulated voices.

Madeline found the ritual and decorum grimly amusing. It seemed in ironic contrast with the violent people she had found the Copelands to be. She remained standing primly waiting for the receptionist to return. She felt she had made the proper impression on him and hoped she would do as well with Thomas Copeland—if she managed to see him.

At last the elderly man in the Prince Albert returned and said haughtily, "Will you come along with me?"

Meekly she followed him.

They passed through a swinging door, then crossed the outer office area to a narrow corridor with doors off it, and halted before one with "James Copeland, Vice President," printed on it in black letters.

"This gentleman will see you," he said, knocking on the door and opening it at the request of a voice inside which she recognized as belonging to Thomas Copeland's other son.

She stepped inside timidly with her heart beginning to pound in earnest. It was a long, narrow office and James' desk was at the extreme end of it. She made her way to the desk and stood uneasily before him.

James Copeland did not bother to rise but greeted her with a cold glare. After he had sized her up, he said, "My father is in conference so I have taken it on myself to interview you."

"Thank you, sir," she said politely.

"You are rather young to be seeking this post," James Copeland announced in his arrogant way. "My grandmother is an old and frail woman. She needs assistance in walking because of a hip injury which has not properly healed."

"I looked after my own grandmother during her illness," she said. "I'm strong and able to help lift an invalid."

James was wearing a dark business suit with a high, hard collar and gray silk tie. He stared at her rather intently as if he'd suddenly recognized her. Then he actually terrified her by saying, "Haven't I seen you somewhere before?"

"No," she said hastily. "This is my first time away from Portland, Maine."

He continued to stare at her. "Odd! You suggest someone to me and yet I can't remember who."

"I have a common face. It often reminds people of someone they know," she said in a desperate attempt to convince him that his impression had been quite normal.

"Can you read?" James snapped coldly at her.

"Yes," she said. "I read very well."

"That is good," he said. "There are girls up here from the country who can neither read nor write, you know."

She found his icy, patronizing manner revolting and thought how unhappy it would be if she were really a little country girl seeking work, instead of playing this charade. A charade by which she hoped to even her score with the Copelands.

She said, "My grandmother was fond of Dickens. I read her most of his works."

James Copeland compressed his thin lips. "The position requires you to go to an island off Cape Cod very shortly. We are moving there for the spring, summer and fall."

"I would not mind that."

He warned her, "We won't have you traipsing back and forth to Boston either. We do have to come to the city twice a week on business, but we do not make any provision for our help to return until we make the transfer back to Brookline at the end of the season."

"It will not matter to me, sir," she said. "I have no relatives or friends in Boston. I have only just arrived here."

He frowned. "Where are you staying?"

She was in a panic for a moment, since she hadn't thought of any answer for this one. "I'm in a boarding house for young ladies operated by a Methodist friend of my mother's," she improvised.

He nodded approvingly. "That sounds like a proper place. I must say you seem ideal for the position except that you are so young."

"I'm in my mid-twenties, sir," she said. "Most of my friends are married with children of their own."

"True," he agreed. "I wish that my father were free to make a decision about you. I usually allow him to have the final word on these things."

She began to worry that he might ask her to return or offer to send a message to her purely imaginary boarding house.

She said, "I promise you if you give me the job I'll work very hard."

Before James Copeland could reply to this, the door of his office was opened without warning and Raymond Copeland, in a top hat and carrying a walking stick, came bursting in. He marched down the office without removing his hat. She saw that he had visibly aged in a few months, with deep lines around his mouth; he had been drinking, she surmised.

He came up beside her and addressed himself to his brother. "What do you mean having my account closed at the Parker House?" he demanded.

James Copeland now rose. He told his brother, "We can discuss that later. Can't you see I'm busy now?"

"I want an answer at once!" an irate Raymond said. "I have had the ignominy of having to turn for assistance to pay my bill to a friend who was my guest. And you are responsible for placing me in the predicament!"

James raised a hand to silence him. "It was Father's decision. Take it up with him!"

Raymond scowled. "You were part of it, I'm sure." Then he glanced at her. "Who is this?"

James spoke for her. He said with controlled anger, "She has nothing to do with you. I'm discussing hiring her to care for our grandmother."

Raymond stood there swaying slightly and a smile spread across his face. "I say we should hire her on the grounds that she is pretty," he declared.

"We were doing nicely until you interrupted us," James told the handsome, drunken man.

Raymond at once reached for his top hat as if in sudden remembrance and took it off. He bowed and said, "Sorry I intruded. Best of luck to you." He donned his hat again and left.

James stood there still in a rage. Then after a moment he said, "Now let me see, where was I?"

"You were explaining the rules of employment to me if I were taken on as your grandmother's companion."

"An, yes," James said, touching a hand to his tie in a nervous gesture. "That was my brother whom you met just now. He will also be at our island residence."

"It sounds most inviting to me," she told him.

James seemed startled by this reply and stared at her. "So you still want the job?"

"Yes," she said.

"Very well," he said in a surprising show of decision for him. "I shall hire you."

"Thank you!" she said, pretending gratitude. She could hardly believe her luck. Not only was she being hired but neither Jim Copeland nor a drunken Raymond had recognized her. It was more than she'd hoped for.

He bent at his desk and quickly wrote some words on a sheet of paper which he handed her. "There you are," he said. "That is the time of our departure on the train for Cape Cod next Friday morning. When we reach our destination by rail we take a boat to Pirate Island and our Dark Harbor home. You can meet us at the railway depot."

"Very well," she said.

"I shall have your ticket purchased and do not bring more than one valise with you. We can't be bothered with too much servants' baggage."

"One valise holds all my things nicely," she said.

The cold James nodded brusquely. "Be obedient and work hard and you'll get along well."

"Thank you, sir," she said with a kind of curtsy she felt the girl she was portraying might make and which she hoped would please him.

102

It evidently did since he added, "It may be if you are diligent you can progress to a more important post in the household. My wife, Alice, has charge of the domestics, and there are several on the staff she is thinking of dismissing."

"I'm most grateful for the opportunity and your interest," she said, smiling broadly. In her exultation over fooling him so completely, she was beginning to enjoy the role.

"Very well," he said with a final nod of dismissal.

She turned and hurried out of the office unable to believe her good fortune. She had managed the first step in her scheme without the least effort. But she sobered quickly as she realized this was only a beginning. The most difficult part of her plan for revenge lay ahead. And with every succeeding move she made, the danger would increase.

Theatre manager Sam Elder was one of those to point this out when he called at the cottage a few days later. He saw her preparations for leaving with the Copeland family as the beginning of a hazardous undertaking and he did not hesitate to tell her so.

Standing and puffing one of his favorite black cigars in her parlor, he warned her, "You are deliberately placing yourself in a circle of danger."

"I know," she said.

"These are a cold group of people and one of them is a would-be murderer."

"I'm also aware of that," she assured him.

Sam's ugly face showed bewilderment. "Is it worth so much to you to get back at them in this way?"

"Yes."

"Suppose you are exposed and the plan backfires on you?"

"I shall at least have tried," she said. "And you forget I'll have a few people in the group whom I can trust. The old woman for whom I'm to act as companion to name one, also Raymond, and, when he is present, Hudson Strout."

"Strout will do what he can," Sam agreed. "I can't vouch for the others. I still think you should concentrate on getting back into the theatre and forget all this. You're not able to sing, but you could do an acting part."

Her smile was bitter as she got up and placed a hand on his arm. "Your concern is appreciated but I cannot change my plans now."

He shrugged. "In that case there's little I can do but wish you luck."

The night before she was to leave with the Copelands she had a recurrence of the awful nightmare in which the black-hooded phantom attacked her. She wakened from the dream terrified and streaming with perspiration. And she began to worry that perhaps Sam and Mrs. Ennis were right, that she was taking too much risk in going to Dark Harbor. Yet at the same time she knew nothing could change her mind.

She was at the railway depot at the appointed time the next morning. The carriage which had brought her in from the suburbs had, at her request, stopped discreetly a block away from the station. She had quickly paid the driver and then carried her rather heavy valise to the busy depot.

Trainmen were calling out the departures of various trains and there were lines of people at several exits leading to the tracks. She stood amid the confusion of the bustling station not knowing which way to go.

Suddenly a voice at her right said, "You are looking for the Copeland party, aren't you?"

She turned and saw it was Raymond and at his side there was a smiling, pretty chestnut-haired girl. Raymond was dressed in brown with a brown tweed hat and the young woman, obviously his latest fiancée, Ann Gresham, was wearing a smart fawn outfit.

She said, "Yes. I'm to join Mrs. Martha Copeland as her companion."

Raymond's eyes twinkled. "So James took my advice and hired you after all. Good, come along with us." He picked up her bag.

They led the way and she followed a respectful step behind them. Madeline was suddenly very uneasy, so near to Raymond, that her disguise was inadequate and he would at any moment see through it. Yet she knew this was largely nerves, as she'd even been able to deceive Sam Elder.

They reached one of the lines and she saw James Copeland standing by a wheelchair in which the ancient Martha Copeland sat. Madeline was alarmed to see how much more frail the old woman had grown in the time since she'd seen her last. The stout Alice was also there giving irate instructions to two of the servants. Juliet stood by, clutching a large handbag, a sullen expression on her lovely face.

Raymond put down the bag and with a smile told Madeline, "You'll have no trouble now." And he moved over with the girl on his arm to talk to Juliet.

His father, Thomas Copeland, appeared out of the circle of people and sternly approached her. He looked more patrician than ever in his dark coat and black top hat. He removed his hat and nodded to her.

"You are the young person whom my son hired to act as companion to my mother?" he said.

"Yes." She felt that she hated him more than all the rest. He was the one who attempted her murder. She was sure of that.

He was staring at her hard. "Have we not met before?"

"No." She felt herself tense as she underwent his close scrutiny.

"Your face has a familiar look but I cannot place you," he declared. "What is your name?"

"Mary Ryan," she said. She had decided on a name with her own initials as some of her clothing was marked with an M.R.

"And you're from Portland, Maine?"

"Yes."

"Very well," he said. "You will sit with my mother on the train. We'll be taking her aboard shortly. And you will keep close to her all the time and see to her needs."

"Yes, sir," she said respectfully.

"Watch your valise," he warned her. "Here is your ticket."

The next several minutes were filled with the confusion of getting through the gate and making her way to the proper track. She followed the others to the long train bound for the Cape and got aboard. She found Martha Copeland, who had been carried on the train ahead of them, already in her seat waiting for her.

The frail old woman's eyes had lost none of their brightness though she had failed in other ways. After Madeline had managed to get her bag up on the rack, she came to the old woman and sat down by her with a smile.

"I'm Mary Ryan," she said.

Martha nodded. "I've been expecting you. They think I'm so decrepit these days that they must have someone to watch me constantly."

"I look forward to being with you."

The old woman's eyebrows shot up with surprise. "You sound as if you really mean that."

"I do."

"That's something I wasn't expecting," the old woman admitted. "I'd planned on how I was going to make your work more difficult. Now you've thrown me off-guard."

She smiled. "I've been looking forward to this and to a stay at Dark Harbor."

"Have you visited Dark Harbor before?" the old woman asked.

"No."

"I think you will like it," Martha Copeland said. "It is quaint and unspoiled. We have a fine big house on a hilltop overlooking the city and harbor. My late husband built it and the family makes a pilgrimage there every year to mark the occasion of his death. It happened on this very weekend fifteen years ago."

"I'm sorry," she said.

The old woman waved this idea aside with a frail hand. "It is no longer a sad occasion for us. We return to open up the house for the season. For the rest of the summer the men will commute back and forth between Dark Harbor and Boston."

"It must take a lot of work to get the house ready," she ventured.

"After being closed for the winter," Martha Copeland agreed. "Some of the servants went ahead and will have things pretty well in order for us."

Their conversation was interrupted as the train started. The car jerked forward with a puff of steam and then the sound of the steadily mounting rhythm as it gained speed. They passed from the grayness of the station out into the open, moving quickly through a section of the old city ribboned with many tracks for incoming and outgoing trains.

"Have you met all the family?" Martha asked above the sound of the train.

"Yes, most of them. There was a girl with your grandson, Raymond, whom I haven't been introduced to as yet."

The old woman grimaced. "Ann Gresham, English music-hall type. Most unsuitable girl for Raymond."

"Oh!" She feigned innocence.

"Yes," Martha Copeland went on. "Raymond is my handsome grandson and he has had many girls want to marry him. Many of them of the wrong sort."

"That's too bad," she sympathized.

"It is especially unfortunate since he was engaged to a very nice French girl, an actress by the name of Madeline Renais. Have you ever heard of her?"

"I'm afraid not," she said carefully. "I lived in a small village outside Portland and rarely had a chance to see any theatre."

"Madeline Renais was a favorite in Boston," the old woman went on happily. "She starred in a number of revues. Raymond saw her and fell in love with her. He brought her to our house in Brookline to stay until their wedding day. I became very fond of her, but the rest of the family felt she wasn't socially suitable to marry a Copeland."

"And was this true?"

"It was poppycock!" Martha said in a disgruntled tone. "Madeline Renais was a person of talent and great poise. She would have done the family credit."

Pretending ignorance of all this, she said, "But the marriage didn't take place?"

"No," the old woman sighed. "I became ill with pneumonia. They all thought I would die, but I pulled through although I was ill for a long while. When I was myself again the first person I asked for was Madeline Renais, and I was told she had gone."

"Gone?"

"Yes," the old woman said, gazing at the open countryside through which the train was passing. "I asked where and I was told a most extraordinary story."

"Indeed?"

Martha nodded. "It seems that Raymond and the girl had a minor quarrel about something. She quickly put on her things and left the house in the middle of a big snowstorm. She didn't return or even send a message. My son, Thomas, had her belongings sent to the theatre where she'd been employed. And still she sent him no message. She simply dropped out of our lives."

"How strange!"

"I thought so," she agreed. "I spoke directly to Raymond about it, since he was the one who was supposed to have married the girl. I found him strangely evasive. He maintained that she had hurt his pride and that he would not go looking for her. I could not understand this then nor do I now."

Madeline raised her eyebrows. "Surely he would have tried to seek her out if he truly loved her?"

"I think he loved her all right," the old woman said. "But I also think something else was troubling him. Something he could not tell me. I have no idea what it might have been, but that was my feeling."

"And now he has this other girl."

"He went to France for his health," the old woman said. "And he met Ann there. She is not nearly the lady Madeline Renais was but, as usual, he seems infatuated with her. If I didn't know him better, I'd say he was a shallow young man. But I know he isn't. I think he plunged into this romance to drown his unhappiness over Madeline Renais."

She was touched by the old woman's words. "You must have liked the Renais girl a great deal."

"I did," Martha Copeland agreed. "And I was sorry she left when I was too ill to speak with her. Had I been myself, things might have turned out very differently."

"Indeed, they might have," Madeline said, thinking they would not have tried to murder her had the old

109

woman been alert at the time.

"And now Raymond is planning to marry this other girl and the family is in the same stew again. I'm sick of Thomas and his ideas of grandeur. His father was never like that."

"I hope it all turns out well," she said.

"I doubt if it will," the old woman sighed. "They'll find some way to make this Ann leave just as they did that other poor girl."

"Perhaps your grandson will not allow that."

"My grandson is not strong in these matters," the old woman told her. And she added, "I'm weary—I've talked too long. I'm going to sleep for a little." Saying this she closed her eyes and within a surprisingly short time had sunk into a deep sleep.

Madeline sat back and thought about the strange conversation in which she had rather objectively discussed herself. At least she'd been right in one thing—Martha Copeland had always been on her side. The confirmation of this was warming. She was sitting thinking about these things and staring straight ahead when Thomas Copeland came down the aisle, steadying himself against the motion of the train by gripping the ends of the seats.

He halted by her and bent down slightly to ask, "Is my mother all right?"

"Yes," she said. "She's having a little sleep." She didn't like his being so near and the glitter in his pale blue eyes made her especially uneasy.

"Very good," he said. "We'll reach the end of our train journey in another hour. Then we'll take the ferry."

He moved on and she felt a distinct relief. There was a strangeness in him beyond his coldness which she felt to be very unhealthy. It seemed to her that he must be touched with madness to have done what he did to her. Likely he was guilty of similar offenses and his conscience must bear a great burden of guilt. Indeed, that was what his manner suggested, a man living under the shadow of his wickedness.

Changing from the train to the ferry was another complicated task. This time she shared some of the responsibility of seeing Martha Copeland safely transferred. The other servants were helpful in spite of Alice's continual nagging and at last the ferry began the thirty-mile voyage to Pirate Island.

Martha Copeland sat in her wheelchair in one of the cabins with Madeline remaining near her. The day was fine and the sea calm.

"I have made the crossing when it was stormy," the old woman confided to her. "It can be very bad. Once I thought we wouldn't make the mainland safely."

"But you do like it on the island?"

"One of my favorite places," Martha Copeland said. "And I'm sure you're going to find it interesting as well."

"I know that I will," she said with a meaning that the old woman could not comprehend.

"It's a fine day if a little cool. Don't let me keep you in this stuffy cabin," Martha said. "Go out on deck and enjoy a look at the ocean."

"I don't want to leave you," she protested.

"Nonsense! I'm used to being alone," the old woman said. "When we reach Dark Harbor I can't expect you to be at my side every second. You've been hired as my companion and not as my shadow."

She smiled at the matriarch's common sense and decided to take advantage of her offer. After making sure that her charge was comfortable she made her way on deck and stood by the railing. The ferry was moving swiftly through the blue water and at this moment there was only a thin line of the mainland still in sight. Otherwise they could have been miles at sea.

Someone stepped up to the railing beside her, and she turned to see that it was a smiling Raymond. He said, "Well, you've managed to avoid being lost thus far."

She smiled wanly in return. "I'm with Mrs. Copeland now. It was just that I wasn't used to such a large railway station and I wanted to locate your party."

"I think you're an excellent addition to our group," he said, studying her.

His close scrutiny made her feel panicky. She felt sure that at any moment he would burst out with her real name. She said, "This is my first position as a servant. In fact I haven't ever worked for anyone before. I lived with my grandmother in Portland and kept house for her."

"Without your glasses you'd be much more attractive," he said, his eyes still on her.

She blushed. "I need them. I'm very shortsighted."

"A pity," he said. "And your voice interests me. You have a very odd voice, low and strangely hoarse."

"I had a throat injury when I was a child," she said. "It left me like this."

Raymond looked at her with good humor. "I wouldn't worry about it," he said. "It makes you more interesting. How are you making out with my grandmother?"

"She's a wonderful old woman," she said.

"I agree. It's too bad her health is failing so rapidly. And I'm glad she has someone to look after her."

"I'll do my best," she said.

"I wouldn't mind having you as my nurse," he said. "I don't see why she should complain."

The situation was becoming difficult and she wished that she could somehow escape him. She was about to make the first move when Ann Gresham arrived, her chestnut hair blowing beneath her wide-brimmed hat, and an irate look in her hazel eyes.

"So this is where you are?" she said sharply to Raymond.

"I came out for some air," he told her.

"Really?" she said, with a meaningful look in Madeline's direction.

Raymond looked embarrassed and said, "This young lady and I just happened to meet. Purely an accident. She has been hired to be my grandmother's companion. Her name is Mary Ryan. Mary, this is my fiancée, Ann Gresham."

"How do you do," she said quietly.

Ann merely gave her an arrogant nod and told Raymond, "You come along with me. I have some things to say to you!"

She turned away from them as they walked off arguing, only too conscious that they were probably quarreling about her. She had suffered a good deal during the time Raymond had been with her and she wondered what he'd say if he knew he'd been talking to Madeline Renais!

She promised herself to keep out of his way as much as possible. She had an idea that it would not take him too long to penetrate her disguise. His conversation with her had made her extremely uneasy.

She walked along the deck in the opposite direction from the other two. It was early in the season and there were few people on the ferry. It was a large boat and the absence of passengers was very noticeable. Moving along the deck she came face to face with a strolling James Copeland, fat, sullen Alice on his arm.

Alice at once halted and demanded, "Why aren't you with my husband's grandmother?"

She said, "Mrs. Copeland pressed me to come out here for a while."

113

Her red, sour face registered fresh annoyance. "That old woman doesn't always know what is best for her. I wouldn't leave her alone long if I were you!"

"I won't," she promised, but she would not return at once to please the overbearing woman.

James Copeland's thin face showed uneasiness. "We can go in and visit Grandmother while Miss Ryan is having a constitutional." And they moved on.

Annoyed at the stout woman's attitude, she took the steps to the upper deck to find some solitude there. And it seemed her chances were excellent, for as far as she could see the upper deck was completely deserted. Once again she went to the railing to stare down at the ocean far below. It was a rather dizzying experience. The ferry cut through the water neatly leaving frothy waves in its wake.

She began thinking about her encounter with Raymond and what it was all leading to. In her valise were the wig, makeup and costume she planned to use, in playing her own ghost. She hoped she would have the courage to carry through her plan successfully and bring Thomas Copeland to justice.

All at once a chill ran down her spine. And she felt isolated and in danger. She had been leaning over the railing and now she was suddenly frightened, terrified by an unknown fear. She whirled around to find Thomas Copeland standing directly behind her, an evil look on his hatchet face and his hands raised as if he'd been about to push her over the railing!

CHAPTER SEVEN

Thomas Copeland instantly lowered his hands and with a guilty look on his cold face said, "I trust I haven't frightened you."

She stood with her back to the railing, gripping it with her outstretched hands. "As a matter of fact you did," she told him, still shaken by what she'd thought was an attempt to shove her overboard. She'd moved just in the nick of time.

"I was startled by the way you turned," he said, "so I raised my hands. It must have looked peculiar to you."

"It did," she said evenly.

"I'm extremely sorry," he said. "I ought to have made my presence known so as not to frighten you."

"I didn't hear you at all," she replied. "I sort of sensed there was someone behind me."

The austere head of the Copeland family said, "Thank goodness no harm was done."

She felt he was merely pretending and had meant to send her toppling over the railing. If he had, the chance of her fall being noticed would have been slight. She would have drowned in the wake of the fast-moving ferry and no one would have missed her until they were ready to disembark. It was a shattering thought.

She shuddered. "I'm cold up here," she said. "I think I'll go back down."

"It is rather chilly," the man in black agreed.

She left him standing by the railing, a strange look on his thin face—a look of frustration, tinged with fear. If his plan had been to hurl her overboard, he had failed and at the same time had betrayed himself as a murderer.

She reached the lower deck and began walking back to the stateroom where she'd left Martha Copeland. A new thought worried her: Had she failed in her disguise? Was it possible that Thomas Copeland had recognized her and so hastily decided to finish the job he'd begun on that winter night months ago when he'd left her to die in the snow?

If so she was in even greater danger than she'd expected. While she was playing ghost and trying to frighten him and whoever else might be guilty into revealing themselves, he might be playing his own cat-and-mouse game of attempting to murder her. She didn't want to believe that he had guessed her identity, but it was a possibility.

Troubled by all this she went back into the cabin and rejoined the old woman in the wheelchair. She stayed with Martha Copeland until the ferry docked at Dark Harbor. As she waited for someone to help her with the invalid, she had her first glimpse of the docks and the main street of the old town which rose steeply from the wharf area.

The houses and shops were just as weathered and gray as the wharves. There were carriages and wagons waiting for passengers and freight. And she began to wonder how far the Copeland family mansion might be from the dock.

Martha Copeland looked up from her chair and answered this question, as if it had been asked her aloud. She said, "We have a twenty minute drive to the house. It sits high on a hill overlooking the town and harbor beyond."

The Copeland family gathered near the opening where the broad planks were flung down in place joining the ship with the wharf. A middle-aged man with a red goatee and wearing a cap with a visor came down the gangway and tipped his hat to Thomas Copeland.

"Welcome back, sir," he said in a lilting voice.

"Thank you," the cold-visaged head of the family replied. He turned to Madeline and said, "This is Jethro Winter. He will see my mother safely ashore and drive you to the house."

Jethro at once smiled and greeted Martha Copeland and expertly navigated her wheelchair up the gangway. A carriage was close by on the wharf, and without hesitation Jethro lifted the invalid woman from the wheelchair up to a seat in the open carriage. Then he helped Madeline up beside the old woman and placed the wheelchair on the opposite seat.

He told them, "There's two other carriages and a wagon to bring along the others and the baggage. We won't have to wait for them." Having made this announcement, he got up into the driver's seat and off they drove along the main street.

Martha settled back against the horsehair seat of the rig and said, "It's good to be back. I'm glad to see the last of Brookline for a while after all the trouble we had there."

"You make it sound most unpleasant," she said.

"It was," the old woman sighed. "My illness and then that girl leaving and upsetting the household more. I'm sure my grandson is still in love with her though he pretends he isn't. His interest in this Ann Gresham doesn't seem sincere to me."

Madeline leaned against the arm of the seat as the carriage wheels rolled along the cobblestone street causing the vehicle to rock a little. She said, "He has asked this girl to marry him."

"It will never be," the old woman predicted.

"Why do you say that?"

Martha looked grim. "I'm certain of it. My son, Thomas, doesn't approve of the match. He always finds means to look after such situations."

"Really?" she said. And her private thought was that this did not surprise her. He had taken care of her very neatly—at least he thought that he had.

Martha's thin face showed interest as she pointed out a two-story building on a corner of the steep street. She said, "That's the Green Heron, the Kimble family owns and operates it as a tavern and hotel."

"It's quite imposing for a small town," she said.

"They say it was built with money made from black gold," Martha said bleakly.

"Black gold?"

"Yes. People think the father of these Kimbles was a captain in the slave trade. Of course no one can say for sure, but that's the rumor. The Kimbles aren't too popular in town, but they do a good enough business I'm told."

Madeline noted a number of different shops along the street, and asked, "Are most of the business establishments located along here?"

"All of them," the old woman said. "New ones are built every year. The town of Dark Harbor is growing fast."

They finally turned along an elm-lined street to the left for a quarter mile until they came to two stone columns guarding a private roadway. Jethro turned the carriage in and after a moment they emerged from the road to open lawns and a giant mansion fronted by great Greek columns. It at once reminded Madeline of pictures she had seen of fine Southern mansions.

She said, "It looks like a house transported from the old South."

Martha Copeland smiled. "My late husband was of Southern ancestry. He built the house in this style because of his great interest in Virginia and the houses there."

"It is a showplace," she said, admiring the great red brick structure with its windows and doors trimmed in white to match the great columns fronting it.

"Thomas considers it an abomination," Martha answered with a wan smile. "But as you have no doubt discovered, my only son is rather severe in his judgements."

Madeline made no reply to this as Jethro came to take them and the wheelchair down from the carriage. A groom came to take the horses and carriage around to the back, while Jethro remained to wheel Martha Copeland into the house.

He lifted the chair up onto the broad platform at the front of the house with ease. The door opened and a pleasant-looking older woman in the black dress and white apron of a servant greeted them. Martha introduced her as Mrs. Matthews, the housekeeper.

The reception hall was spacious and cool. Jethro pushed the wheelchair down a broad corridor which ran to the rear of the house. At last they came to an open door on the left and he wheeled her into a pleasant parlor.

He nodded to the old woman with his hat in hand. "You'll be all right now, Mrs. Copeland."

"Thank you, Jethro," she said. "It is good to see you again."

"And to see you, Ma'am," he answered with a smile. "Winters are mighty lonesome here."

"I can imagine," she said. "I'll be looking to see how you have made out with the gardens."

His lined face shadowed a little. "Don't be too critical, Ma'am. It's been a backward season."

"I won't," she promised. "But I am anxious to take a look around."

"Yes, Ma'am," he said. And with a bow to her and Madeline, he left the room.

"Jethro has a long record of service here," Martha told her. "He really loves this place and he supervises the garden work along with other duties."

"He seems very nice," she agreed.

"Your room will be directly across the hall from here," the old woman informed her. "I decided to live on this ground floor as it allows me easy access to all the large rooms and I have a ramp at one of the rear doors which takes me out onto the grounds without the problem of steps. I hope you don't mind having a ground-floor room."

"It makes no difference at all," she said, as indeed it didn't. For her purposes one room was as good as another.

"I have most of my meals here in my suite," the old woman explained. "So you will eat here with me as I dislike eating alone."

"I understand," she said.

"On rare occasions I go to the dining room and join the others but such times are becoming few and far between. I often find the talk at the table too upsetting. The family is given to argument."

The wagon soon arrived with their things and Madeline was kept busy unpacking. By the time she finished she was exhausted. Her own room was rather small and its two windows faced the gardens. The suite which the old woman occupied had a living room and a bedroom with several large closets off it. There was a tiny, general utility room equipped as a kitchen at the left through an archway.

When she completed storing away the old woman's belongings, she went to her own small room and quickly unpacked the valise which she'd brought with her. At the very bottom of it were the wig and other implements she planned to use in her disguise. She stood on a chair and placed these items far back on a high shelf in the single closet. She'd barely gotten down and put the chair back in place when James Copeland knocked on her door. Seeing James, she waited for him to explain his visit.

He stared at her rather strangely as he inquired, "Did you get your luggage safely?"

"Yes," she said, standing with her hand on the door knob. "I had only one valise. You had instructed me to travel lightly."

"Then everything is all right. You are happy in your room?" he said, rather flustered.

"It seems very adequate."

"I will let my father know you are satisfied," the prim, young man said. "If you have any complaints speak to my wife."

"Very well," she said, feeling certain the bad-tempered Alice would pay scarce attention to any problems she might have.

James lingered in the doorway a moment longer as he said, "I trust you feel at home here." And then he turned and vanished down the hallway.

She closed the door after him, thinking that he was a strange young man. His mention of her being happy in the house made her stop and consider what her feelings were towards it. She'd only been at Pinecrest a short while so it was hard to say whether she felt more at ease here than she had in the Copeland's Brookline mansion.

In Brookline she had come to fear and hate her surroundings and most of the people in the house. Fright was perhaps her main memory of the period she'd lived there. This house was also large and shadowed and she'd seen little of it. But the people in it were the same who had made her existence one of living terror in Brookline. This time she hoped to bring tenor to some of them.

She assumed that while she had been unpacking the rest of the family had arrived and were settling into their various rooms. She could not help but wonder where Raymond and his new fiancée might be in the house. Without a question they would have rooms on one of the upper floors where the bedrooms were located.

She was satisfied to be separated from the others. It would make it easier both to play ghost and to avoid the rest of the family, especially Raymond. She continued to worry that perhaps both he and Thomas Copeland had seen through her disguise. The incident on the upper deck of the ferry had made her doubly suspicious.

Now she went back to the plain dresser in her room and checked the various drawers. Everything was neatly put away. And in the upper left drawer she'd placed her more personal items such as a box containing earrings, a favorite book of poetry, another velvet box with two prized bracelets, and an engraved gold watch which she sometimes wore around her neck. Having made an inventory of all these valuables she closed the drawer and left the room.

"My appetite is always better here," old Martha Copeland declared as she pushed aside her empty dessert dish and prepared to enjoy her coffee.

Seated at the small table with her, Madeline said, "Your cook here is excellent, much better than in Brookline." The words escaped her before she could censor them. At once she hated herself for being a fool.

The old woman's thin face took on an alert look. "How would you know that?"

She hesitated, quickly trying to decide how to correct her mistake, and finally answered, "I mean your cook must be better here if you enjoy the food more." And she hoped this would satisfy the invalid.

Martha Copeland seemed to consider this. Then she said, "I can understand your assuming that. I thought perhaps someone had mentioned it to you. As a matter of fact the cook here is far superior to the one in Brookline. But I don't give full credit to her for my improved appetite. I think it has something to do with the change of atmosphere and the sea air on this island."

"That could well be," she said.

"In Brookline I live on an upper floor and that makes it much more difficult for me," the old woman went on.

"I'd say the arrangement here is ideal," Madeline said.

"Yes. There are only the servants' rooms to the other side of us and it is quiet."

Madeline remained with the old woman for a while after the evening meal until Martha complained of being tired, and then helped her into bed.

The old woman said, "There is no need for you to stay with me any longer. I won't need you until morning."

"You're certain?" she asked.

"Yes," Martha Copeland assured her. "The maid will be in later with fresh water and she'll put out the lamp for me. You can come get me ready for breakfast at eight."

"Very well," she said.

"In the meantime, get to know the place," the old woman said. "It's still light out and it ought to be pleasant if a little on the cool side. Explore the grounds and the rest of the house. You are not restricted to servants' quarters, you know."

Madeline was pleased to take advantage of the old woman's offer. She went out into the garden by a rear door only a short distance from her room. She noted that this exit would make an excellent passage for her when she assumed her ghost role. As she strolled along the gravel path of the garden she was impressed by the ornate flower beds and the high green hedges which served to set apart sections of the area.

There was a square summerhouse with a floor raised

above ground level, a roof and latticed sides. Vines grew up the lattice work, giving the small structure a pleasant look and adding to its privacy. It was quite a distance from the main house and beyond a row of hedges.

Twilight was settling as she approached, and suddenly she heard a woman sobbing. It clearly came from the square structure. She hesitated by the hedge and a moment later saw Raymond come striding out of the open entrance and down the steps. He looked neither to left nor right, but set a straight course for the main house. He passed close by her without seeing her.

Madeline waited a little and then the woman's sobbing came clearly again. She walked slowly across to the structure and after a slight hesitation, mounted the steps and looked in. It was dark inside, but she was able to see Ann Gresham seated on a bench crying bitterly.

She felt a sincere sympathy for the unhappy woman who was almost precisely in the same position in which she herself had been those long months ago. There could be no doubt that the Copeland family was making it difficult for her and that Raymond was being as obtuse as usual.

She took a step closer to the girl who had not noticed her approach. In a tentative voice, she asked, "Is there anything I can do to help?"

Ann Gresham's reaction was sharp. She looked up at her and in a shocked voice, declared, "How dare you interfere! Get away from here you—you servant!"

"I'm sorry," she apologized to the distraught young woman and quickly left the summer house.

She walked rapidly towards the mansion stung by what the girl had said. She knew that Ann Gresham was probably terribly upset, but she had been very rude to her. As she reached the gardens again it was getting dark. Suddenly she saw a figure walking towards her out of the dusk.

A moment later she recognized Juliet, Raymond's attractive but sullen sister. She came up to her, stopped, then said, "You're taking a look around?"

"Yes," she said. "You have lovely grounds."

"They take a great deal of work," Juliet said in her lofty way. And then she added, "You know I sometimes feel that I've met you somewhere before."

In a taut voice Madeline said, "I think that is not at all likely. I only left Portland a month or so ago."

"Really?" Juliet said in her cold manner. "That is rather interesting. I have friends in Portland."

"Oh!" Madeline was a little aghast since she really knew very little about Portland. She'd simply seized on the name of the city in a hurry when she'd had her interview with James.

"Yes," the other girl said. "I must ask my friends if they know you. Your name is Mary Ryan, am I right?"

"You are right," she said nervously. "But I doubt if I would ever have met them. We'd be apt to travel in different social circles."

"Still you never know, do you?" Juliet said, standing there a blurred figure in the deeping blue shadows.

"I suppose not."

"Did you live in the city or out Cape Elizabeth way?"

"Cape Elizabeth?" she said blankly.

"Come now," Juliet said, "you must know Cape Elizabeth."

"Not well," she quickly replied. "I was brought up in a village at the other end of the city." This was the worst kind of guessing but she hoped this would satisfy the other girl.

"In the Falmouth district?" Juliet asked.

"A little beyond it," she said cautiously. "Just a tiny village you never hear about."

"I see," Juliet said in a rather strange tone which led her to worry that the girl might be suspicious of her.

At that moment a handsome Dalmatian came running up to them. He was large for his breed and at once nuzzled a wet nose in Madeline's hand. She patted his head and knelt a little to speak directly to him. The dog responded to her fondling with happy panting and a wagging tail.

She rubbed the dog's satinlike ears and said to Juliet, "He's lovely. I'm fond of Dalmatians."

"His name is Nero," Juliet said. "He can be a nuisance when he likes."

She stood up still patting the dog's head. "I can't imagine anyone not liking him!"

"He's a family favorite," Juliet agreed in her bored way, and she stretched out a hand to pat the dog. Immediately there was a startling change in the animal.

As Juliet's hand reached for him the big dog began to growl ominously and back away. The hackles at his neck raised and he began to tremble.

Madeline stared at the animal in amazement. "Why is he acting like that?"

"I told you he isn't to be depended upon," Juliet said in an annoyed tone as she withdrew her hand.

The dog continued to stand there growling and trembling. Madeline tentatively approached him and in a soothing voice asked, "What's the matter, Nero?" The dog glanced at her but did not move.

"He's a silly, bad-tempered creature!" Juliet said with utter disgust. "I refuse to waste my time on him!" Then she turned and walked back towards the house.

As soon as the stately blonde girl retreated, the big dog relaxed. He ceased his growling and he allowed her to pat him.

She asked, "What is wrong, Nero? Why did she upset you

so much?" As she asked the question and fondled him, his tail once more began to wag.

She heard a footstep on the gravel path behind her and looked up to see another blurred figure. This time it was a man who had come up in the night shadows to stand by her.

The man spoke and she recognized by his voice that it was the handyman, Jethro, who had met them at the ferry. He said, "I was out here and I couldn't help hearing you and Miss Juliet talking."

"Oh?" She hardly knew what to say.

Jethro took a step closer and patted Nero. The big dog seemed delighted to see him and rubbed his head against him. Jethro said, "I heard what Miss Juliet said about this dog."

"And?"

"You mustn't listen to her," Jethro said, still patting the Dalmatian. "Nero is a fine animal."

"Yet he didn't seem to want her near him. He growled and acted strangely."

"Good reason," the servant said with bitterness. "Miss Juliet has a savage temper. One day she became angry with Nero and took a rake and beat him until he was a mass of cuts and bruises!"

She was shocked. "Juliet did that?"

"Yes, Miss," Jethro said. "You'd be well advised not to cross her. She can be a bad one when she's aroused. Nero won't go near her since that day."

"I can't blame him."

"Nor do I," Jethro said. "It was a cruel display. She acted like a mad creature."

"I had no idea her temper was that uncontrolled. That she'd resort to violence of the kind you describe."

"I've been here some years," Jethro said darkly. "And I've

seen things you wouldn't believe. She was wicked cruel as a child."

"Then this sort of thing is not new with her?"

"No," Jethro said with undisguised contempt. "Once she attacked a little boy who lived in the next house and almost put his eye out."

"How awful!"

"That was only one case," the handyman said. "I could bring up others but I won't. So don't blame Nero for the way he acted, Miss."

"I won't," she said.

Jethro bade her good night and then walked off into the near darkness with Nero trotting happily at his heels. His revelations were startling. She'd never realized that Juliet's coldness could quickly turn to physical violence. She could understand why the pleasant young lawyer, Hudson Strout, had avoided marrying Raymond's blonde sister. From what Hudson had said he was only waiting for a good opportunity to break his engagement to her.

Madeline hoped that Hudson Strout would soon visit the island to see how she was managing. He had been apprehensive about what she was planning to do. It would be awkward for him to appear at the old mansion too often, since he was attempting to cool his relationship with Juliet. But she thought he would undoubtedly put in at least one appearance.

She walked around to the front of the house. Now the yellow amber of lamps had appeared at some of the windows. The porch which ran the length of the house was in darkness and the big white columns rising from it stretched high up into the night. Once again she began to sense the same fear she'd had in Brookline. The same sensations of some unknown threat began to plague her.

Much of it was due to the coldness of the Copelands. They created a frigid, grim atmosphere in whatever house they occupied. But more than that, the concentrated hatred and violence of at least one of them had brought her close to death and changed her entire life.

Now Ann Gresham was about to get the same treatment. Yet the British girl had rebuked her rudely when she'd tried to help. Perhaps the unfortunate girl, like the dog, was in such a panic from cruel treatment that she reacted violently to any sympathetic gesture.

Madeline felt that Ann was doubly unfortunate in that Raymond probably had no sincere love for her. It was all too likely he had turned to Ann Gresham on the rebound and that he would be less considerate of her. Madeline had an idea that once she'd revealed the identity of her attacker and Raymond realized that she was still alive, he would once again pledge his love to her. But a lot of things had to happen before that.

She had to play the role of her ghost and somehow make her assailant reveal himself. She was worried that Thomas Copeland, whom she believed to be the guilty one, already had discovered her identity. She based this on several things, including what had happened on the ferry. If this should be the case she was going to have a difficult task in unmasking him.

She was standing staring into the darkness when she heard the front door open behind her. It was Thomas Copeland who had come out.

He seemed surprised to find her there. In a tone of mild sarcasm he asked, "Are you so fond of being alone in the darkness, Miss Ryan?"

She said, "Sometimes I find it easier to think out problems when I'm alone in the dark."

The gaunt man stood by her. "You have no fear of the dark, then?"

"Not really."

"Most people have," he went on in his cold fashion. "You will hear many stories of ghosts on this island. It is a place of phantoms."

"Oh?"

"Yes. They claim that on stormy nights if you walk up the main street you can hear the music, laughter and loud voices in revelry from taverns which have long ceased to exist. The echoes of the dead!"

"I suppose the island has a long history," she said.

"It was a favorite harbor for pirates a long way back," he said. "Then the Puritans came and soon after them a group of Satanists cast out of England. Not to mention the Quakers and Portuguese who, along with the ordinary Yankees, have welded together to make Pirate Island a sort of melting pot."

She said, "I refuse to believe in ghosts."

He turned to her in the darkness. "That may be most unwise of you. Every old house on this island has its phantom."

"This one as well?"

"Naturally," Thomas Copeland said. "Our ghost is supposed to be the specter of a long dead pirate. He murdered a number of his associates in a hut which stood almost on the very spot where we built. He wore a black hood to conceal his identity. And it is said his cowled ghost can still be seen on certain nights."

A ripple of fear coursed down her spine. He was describing exactly the apparition which had attacked her in Brookline. Was he deliberately playing a game with her? Had he guessed who she was and so was telling her this story to work on her nerves? Or was he being genuine in his account of the phantom?

She said, "I can only trust I have no meeting with your phantom."

He said, "You had best be prepared. His presence is so strong that some of the servants claim he has followed us to our other house near Boston and shown himself there."

Madeline heard this with rising uneasiness. It was all too pat. She felt that Thomas Copeland was setting the circumstances for another attack on her which he would blame on the ghost.

She said faintly, "I think I'll go in now."

"You'll miss the best part of the night," he said, glancing up. "The stars are just beginning to appear. On clear nights they offer a magnificent panorama."

"I'm sure they do," she said nervously, anxious to get away from his calculating, menacing presence. "But I'm weary. It has been a long, tiring day."

"That is true," Thomas Copeland said. "I trust you won't find my mother too much of a strain on you."

"No, I'm going to enjoy being with her," she said.

"I'm glad to hear that," Thomas Copeland replied.

They exchanged goodnights and she went inside and hurried down the long dark corridor to her room. The house was very silent now. Her door creaked as she opened it and went inside. A candle burned in a holder on the dresser. It was the sole light in the modest bedroom.

She stood there in the flickering light gazing at herself in the dresser mirror. Her face loomed out from the background shadows in the glow of the candle, and she realized with a start that in her disguise she was almost a stranger to herself. She could be looking at someone else. The plain blonde girl with spectacles in no way resembled her as she'd once looked.

How could Thomas Copeland or any of the others know her? If they did, it might be from some clues which they'd stumbled on. She'd almost given herself away in talking to the old woman. She had to be wary.

And then a strange feeling came over her. A feeling that someone was in the room with her or had been there in her absence. It struck her with a frightening impact!

CHAPTER EIGHT

For a moment she stood frozen with indecision. The sense of someone else in the room was overwhelming. She slowly turned and stared into the shadows by her bed and could see no sign of anyone. Still unsatisfied she went over to the closet and hesitantly opened its door. Her clothes were still on the hangers as she'd left them and no one was lurking in the rear of the closet.

Then she remembered the items of her disguise and quickly brought up a chair to see that these things were still on the shelf. They were. Puzzled, she got down, went to the dresser and opened the drawers. When she came to the drawer in which she'd placed her jewelry she halted and stared down in it!

The thing which had riveted her attention was the attractive fob watch. She had left it there unopened and now the back of the case was snapped open! And as she gazed at it in alarm, she knew that someone had been rummaging through the dresser and had come upon the watch. And that someone must have opened the back of the case.

With this disclosure came another sickening realization. In the back of the watch there had been a cutout of a magazine pencil sketch of her done by a Parisian artist when she was appearing in a revue. She had clipped it out and fitted it in the back of her watch. With the passing of time she'd forgotten all about it, until now when this incident brought it all back!

Someone in the old mansion now had this sketch of Madeline Renais. And whoever it was must surely know that she was the revue star. Probably Thomas Copeland had searched her room while she was out walking. He already suspected her and this would offer him all the proof he needed. It was a terrifying thought.

With trembling hands she snapped the watch case closed and put it back in the drawer. There was nothing she could do but brazen the situation out. If anyone showed the drawing to her, she would simply maintain that Madeline Renais was a favorite star of hers. That she'd seen the artist's study in a magazine and cut it out to keep as a memento. It was thin but it might get her by if they didn't recognize her.

Trying to comfort herself with this explanation, she began to prepare for bed. Her first day and night on the island had been exhausting, and she was more than ready for sleep. Her role of ghost would have to wait for another and more appropriate time.

Nothing disturbed her sound sleep. She didn't even suffer from dreams of the hooded attacker which so often bothered her. And when she went in to help old Martha Copeland with her morning ablutions, she felt completely rested. The sun was shining and there was the promise of another nice day.

At breakfast the old woman said, "I'd like to go out in the carriage this morning. Not only would I enjoy the ride but I'd like to show you some of the island."

"That would be pleasant," Madeline agreed. She was willing to do anything which would keep her out of the way of Raymond and his grim-faced father.

Martha had the carriage made ready and Jethro came and carried her out to it. Soon they were driving along one of the curving main roads which crisscrossed the island.

"We're driving as far as Gull Lighthouse," the old woman said. "I want you to see the lighthouse and also the monastery along the way."

She was surprised. "They have a monastery on the island?"

"Yes. The monks operate a leper hospital there, though they don't have a lot of patients now." And she went on to give her a fascinating account of the place and how it came to be built. As they drove by the great buildings of stone on a hill overlooking the ocean, she saw some monks in their brown habits toiling in the fields.

They went on to the lighthouse and Jethro brought the carriage to a halt while she stepped down from it and strolled across to the edge of the cliffs. Jethro walked with her and explained various things about the island. He told her of the days when whaling was the main business of the islanders. Of how in 1791 the ship *Beaver* rounded Cape Horn and with rich profits to her owners opened the sperm hunting grounds of the Pacific. After that, he said, for more than two generations the Dark Harbor men lived on the Pacific Ocean except for brief vacations at home, and it was from the sea that they brought back the wealth which made the town and island prosperous.

On the drive back, Martha Copeland told her that in the old days Dark Harbor was actually run by women—an unheard-of thing anywhere else, but a necessity here, since all the men were away at sea on whaling expeditions.

Madeline thoroughly enjoyed the excursion and felt better for getting away from the gloomy old mansion. On their return, Martha Copeland went to her room for a rest and she had some free time to herself.

She was wearing a white dress and carrying a white parasol as protection from the warm afternoon sun. Once again she walked as far as the summerhouse and since it was empty she went inside and sat in its cool shade. She was able to watch what was taking place on the grounds through open windows in the lattice work.

In the distance Raymond and Ann were playing croquet. She watched them for a while and saw that after each game Raymond went up to the girl and showed some slight sign of affection. Sometimes he would place an arm around her, at others he would applaud her play, or just stand chatting intimately with her. It seemed apparent that they had patched up their quarrel of the previous night.

She did not find this surprising as she recalled her own stormy romance with Raymond. Wearying of watching them, she sat back on the bench of the summerhouse in a section where the thick vines growing outside shut off her view and also protected her from the sun. Sitting there with her eyes closed, she suddenly heard voices from the lawn and at once she recognized that it was James and Alice. She remained very still and listened.

"The situation can't go on!" James complained.

"You say that, but what do you propose to do about it?" Alice said acidly.

"I have to let Father decide," James said dejectedly. "He always takes the initiative in these matters!"

"I'd say he's taking a great risk this time. He's been entirely too slow making up his mind," Alice said in her irritable fashion.

"This Ann has to go," James declared. "And we don't want any trouble about it."

"Not any more than last time," Alice said.

"That was a near miss," her husband agreed. "We just managed it. And another time Raymond won't be so easy to handle."

"He's not really in love with this Ann," Alice pointed out. "He's turned to her because he lost his Parisian beauty."

"He took that hard!"

"More's the pity," Alice said with contempt. "Your father has to make up his mind as he did last time. Otherwise we'll soon be faced with a situation beyond our control."

"Raymond always finds quite unsuitable young women and brings them to us," James complained.

Their voices now trailed away and became inaudible, but she had heard enough and fortunately they hadn't been aware of her presence. It had been a shocking experience to hear them coldly discussing getting rid of Ann Gresham and referring to the near disaster they'd had in removing her from the scene. This indicated without any question that the family had banded together in the attack on her and later in disposing of her in that alley.

She was of the opinion that Thomas Copeland had come into her room in that black hood and made the actual attack on her. But when this was done James must have helped him in getting her away from the house. And both Juliet and Alice must have been in on the crime. By Alice's own comment they'd had a hard time convincing Raymond that he'd been jilted. He surely wouldn't accept such an explanation again. So they did have a problem.

Still she was certain they'd find a way. Plotting together they would work some scheme out. She remained in the summerhouse for a little while longer and then left it to walk back across the lawn past the croquet area. Ann Gresham had disappeared and Raymond was still there playing a lone game. He halted when he saw Madeline and, croquet mallet still in hand, came over to greet her.

"Do you play?" he asked.

"Not well," she said.

"Would you care for a game?"

She smiled. "Perhaps just one. I can't leave your grandmother alone too long."

"Don't worry about her," he said. "She sleeps most of the afternoon." He found her a mallet and led her to the first wicket.

She put her parasol aside and devoted her full attention to the sport. It was the first time she and this man whom she'd loved had been alone together since she'd returned to the family. She was nervous and betrayed this by trying too hard and making some bad plays.

"You're much too tense!" he said jokingly. "What earnest young women you Maine girls are!"

She stood back for him to play. "We do take things seriously," she said.

He made a perfect play and as the ball rolled across the grass, he laughed. "There, you see! I do fine and I don't try hard at all."

She glanced at him. "Is that your philosophy of life? Not to try too hard?"

"I suppose it is," he agreed. He was standing close to her and she was conscious of liquor on his breath.

He won the game and insisted that she join him at a table on the patio at the side of the house. There a manservant brought them drinks. She had a fresh lemonade while he ordered something with gin. She was holding her parasol over her head again to keep off the warm sun.

With a knowing smile, she said, "You drink a great deal, don't you?"

He stared at her in surprise. "Have you found that out in such a short time or did someone tell you?"

"A little of both."

His handsome face showed a wry, humorous look. "My grandmother has been filling you in about me."

"Perhaps," she teased him.

He put his glass down and she noticed that his hand trembled noticeably. It worried her.

He studied her questioningly across the table. "What else did she tell you?"

"Many things."

"Tell me some of them."

"You don't really want to know," she said.

"I do," he said, his face shadowing. "I find it interesting to know what the others in the family think of me."

"I don't want to cause trouble."

"There'll be no trouble," he promised. "Tell me what my dear grandmother thinks of me."

She hesitated. "I'm certain she's very fond of you."

"Then she's the only one among them who is," he said with an air of disgust.

"And she worries about your wildness and drinking."

"Sounds familiar," he groaned.

"And she's not happy about this girl you're engaged to," she said, deciding to sound him out while she had the chance.

He frowned. "None of them are."

"She says something like this happened before. That you made up your mind to marry a girl who wasn't at all suitable."

Raymond's face flushed and he stared at her. "Are you sure that she said that?"

"She said your father was beside himself with rage about it. You were engaged to some actress."

"Madeline Renais." He said her name bitterly.

Hearing him speak her name and in that manner gave her an eerie feeling. She tried to hide her upset and said, "I think that was the name."

"She left me you know," he said. "I didn't give her up."

"She didn't tell me the details," Madeline said, hoping to drag some opinion about it from him.

"Madeline ran off one winter night. I've never heard from her since," he said with almost a touch of weariness. "Of course, I didn't try to get in touch with her—I have my pride. If she didn't care any more than that, best to let her go."

"You allowed your pride to keep you from seeking her out? She might have had a good explanation for leaving as she did."

"Never," he said.

"You're not a tolerant person, are you?" she said.

"I have never pretended to be." He lifted his drink again and finished it this time.

She said, "So you've become engaged to this Ann without ever forgetting that other girl?"

He lifted the silver bell on the table and rang it for the manservant as he told her, "I've tried to forget her."

"But you haven't managed to?"

"That's right," he said. The servant came and Raymond ordered another gin while she refused a second lemonade.

She said, "So you plan to marry this British girl?"

"Yes."

"Do you think you'll be happy? I mean with this other girl still on your mind?"

He shrugged. "As happy as most people. How about my brother James and his fat Alice? Do you think that match was made in Heaven? He's frightened of her, I swear."

She managed a smile. "I don't think it's quite that bad."

"I do," he said. The servant came back with his second drink and Raymond gulped down a mouthful at once. Then he stared at her and said, "You're a strange person."

Instantly on guard, she asked, "Why do you say that?"

"I find myself liking you though I don't agree with anything you say."

"Oh?"

140

"I feel easy with you. It's almost as if we'd known each other a long time."

"We've barely met."

"That makes it all the more odd," he said. "Every so often when you say something, you remind me of someone else."

She didn't dare ask him who. Instead she said, "I can safely say you're a stranger to me. I haven't even started to understand you."

"We'll get to know each other before the summer is over," he predicted.

She closed her parasol and stood up. "I must go inside now. Thank you for the game and the drink."

He was on his feet. "My privilege and pleasure," he said with a bow. "And tell my grandmother to stop filling you in on all my weaknesses."

She smiled. "I will. But I can't promise that she'll stop."

"Knowing her I'm sure that she won't," was his retort.

She left him and went inside. The brief interlude with him had left her in a strange mood. She was still greatly attracted to him but now she saw him more objectively and she was not completely enchanted with what she saw. His health had clearly been affected by his constant dissipation. His hands trembled noticeably now, and his attitude of resignation towards most things struck her as a character weakness.

What it amounted to was that she was still fond of him but no longer saw him with the starry eyes she had when she'd first fallen in love with him. Then he had seemed completely charming and she'd respected his background of family and wealth. Now she saw that his charm was perhaps shallow and his character jaded by wealth and position.

She went in to join his grandmother and found the old woman sitting up in bed. Martha informed her, "The maid came by and saw that I was comfortable."

"I'm sorry I'm late coming in," she apologized.

The old woman looked amused. "You have done no harm. I can always call a maid when I need one. I don't want you to be my slave."

"That is kind of you," Madeline answered. "I stopped outside to talk for a little."

The old woman nodded, "Yes I know. You played croquet with my grandson and then sat on the patio with him."

"How do you happen to know all that?" she asked in surprise.

Martha Copeland chuckled. "I know more things than you guess. I have my spies among the servants and I know most of what happens here."

"Well, you were completely informed," she said.

The old woman gave her a serious glance. "One thing. About my grandson Raymond, don't be taken in by him too easily."

Her eyes widened. "Why do you say that?"

"I want to warn you," the old woman said. "He has wrenched far too many female hearts. I don't want you to be another of his victims."

"You can't be serious!" she protested.

"Indeed I am," the old woman said. "Raymond is the most charming of all my grandchildren. But he is not all cake and icing. Don't be deceived."

There was a note of earnestness in Martha Copeland's voice which could not be ignored. Madeline said, "I'll keep that in mind."

"Do," her employer urged. "He worries me and he could be dangerous to you." With that the old lady changed the subject.

Madeline was relieved to end the discussion of Raymond and his failings. She realized that his grandmother was seeing the same flaws in him which were now bothering her. She wondered how long it would take Ann to become critical of him.

The evening passed uneventfully. Just after dark Madeline took a short stroll and heard padding feet behind her. She turned as Nero came bounding up to join her. She patted the big Dalmatian and he pressed against her in his most friendly fashion. Then he heard a sound in the bushes and went running off.

There was a full moon and she decided that this would be her night to begin her plan of revenge on the family. She went back to her room and brought her disguise down from the closet shelf and sat before the dresser mirror to transform herself to a reasonable likeness of Madeline Renais.

It took some time before she was satisfied. She put on the black wig with the long flowing hair and then donned the ghostly white cover-all which she'd brought for this purpose. The effect was very good.

She had no set plan. Her first step was to go out in the moonlight where she might be seen by some member of the Copeland clan. She didn't care which one saw her. It would be enough to start the rumor that her ghost had been seen. After that she would single out individual members to work on.

After waiting until it was reasonably late and the house was quiet, she slipped out of her room in her ghostly make-up and hurried down the short hall to the rear exit. Once she was out in the garden, she moved behind a hedge which gave her a view of the house. The moon was bright enough so she would be seen easily by anyone. She was trembling with nervousness and decided that being a ghost was almost as frightening as seeing one.

She moved slowly, using the hedge as a shelter until she

wished to be revealed. As she came around to the front of the house she saw that most of the windows were dark. But there was still light showing from the living room windows, so someone must be down there late. She stood watching the windows and debating whether she dared venture up to one of them and look in. If anyone inside saw her it would give them a start.

But this presented the problem of making a quick escape before those inside could come out to catch her. As she was considering this move, the front door opened and James and Alice came out, apparently to sample the air before retiring. Her heart began to pound with excitement as she realized the time had come to test her disguise.

As they stood there talking, she edged around the bushes and stood out on the open lawn. Motionless she gazed up at the moon in a ghostly fashion. From the corner of her eye she could see the two on the porch. James had his back partly to her so it was Alice who saw her first.

"Look!" the fat woman screamed, clutching her husband by the arm frantically. "Look!" A second scream cut through the air.

A bewildered James slowly turned and when he saw the spectre his mouth gaped open and he stood there in frozen silence.

"James!" the scream came more faintly from Alice and she collapsed on the porch.

This brought him out of his trance and he knelt down, babbling and imploring his wife to come to. Madeline took the opportunity to dodge behind the hedge again and use its cover to reach the rear lawn and the safety of the back door. She rushed in and down the hall to her room. There she hastily discarded the wig and robe and dabbed cocoa cream on her face to remove the make-up. As she was doing this she heard confusion and loud voices emanating from the front of the house.

She quickly donned her nightgown and robe. Then she put on the spectacles and looked at herself in the mirror. It was the stranger she saw again—the naive, plain girl from Maine. Satisfied, she went out into the hall. She heard Martha Copeland calling fretfully in her bedroom.

Madeline quickly went to her and saw the old woman had already lit a candle in a holder on her bedside table.

"What is the commotion?" Martha demanded.

"I don't know," she said. "I was asleep and it woke me up."

"Help me into my chair and take me out there," the old woman said. "Something dreadful must have happened!"

It took a few minutes and some effort to switch the elderly invalid from her bed into the chair. Then she wheeled her out to the reception hall area. By this time lamps had been lighted and the overweight Alice had been carried into the living room where she now lay stretched out on a sofa. Thomas Copeland with a brandy glass in his hand was sitting beside her. An agitated James stood watching the two, as did Juliet. Only Raymond and Ann were missing. Madeline assumed that they hadn't heard the commotion.

As she wheeled Martha Copeland up to her son, the old woman demanded, "What is the meaning of all this?"

The gaunt Thomas turned to his mother irritably and said, "Alice has had an attack of hysterics. She seems to think she saw a ghost of some sort!"

"A ghost?" Martha Copeland demanded with a strange look on her thin face.

"Nonsense of course," her son said. He turned to the prostrate woman again and said, "Try some more of this brandy." The only reaction from Alice was a groan.

Juliet, in a fancy gold and blue dressing gown, looked disgusted. "How can she be so silly?"

James turned on his sister angrily to defend his wife. "She is not being silly! I saw it too!"

"Saw what?" the old woman demanded.

James looked down at his grandmother in a miserably confused state. "The ghost," he said with effort.

"What ghost?" the old woman persisted.

James licked his thin lips. "You're not going to believe me. We saw the ghost of Madeline Renais! We both saw her!"

From the sofa there came another moan from Alice.

Thomas Copeland glanced up at his son with barely-controlled rage. "That is utter nonsense!"

"No, Father," James said unhappily. "I saw her plainly. I couldn't mistake her. When I turned to help Alice, she vanished."

Martha Copeland eyed him with skepticism. "Who saw this ghost first?"

"Alice," James said reluctantly.

"I thought so," was the old lady's grim reply. "Alice saw something which she took to be the ghost of Madeline Renais and then influenced you into thinking the same thing!"

"No!" James protested.

"It has to be," Juliet said in disgust. "For one thing, as far as we know Madeline Renais is not dead! So how could you have seen her ghost?"

The thin, young man made a futile gesture. "She must be dead. I saw her. Her face was upturned to the moon. I could make out every feature and her long black hair was loose on her shoulders."

"Let us hear no more of that nonsense," Thomas Copeland reprimanded his son. But it was apparent the incident had taken a heavy toll on him. The veins at his temples stood out and his gaunt face was a sickly color.

Martha Copeland nodded. "We can't allow Alice's bad nerves to upset the entire household. Better take her up to bed. She'll feel herself after a sound night's sleep. So will we all!"

Thomas Copeland stood up and nodded to his mother. "You are right. Go back to your room and forget about this. I'll see Alice gets upstairs safely."

James stood there dejected and still too shocked to be of much help. Juliet turned on her heel and with a sigh of disgust made her way to the stairs. Madeline wheeled the old woman's chair out of the room and down the hall. Behind her she could still hear Alice's moaning protests and the men's troubled voices as they got her up from the sofa.

When Martha Copeland was back in bed she declared, "Alice has never been noted for her intelligence, but this seeing ghosts is unbelievable."

Madeline played her part very carefully. She said, "But your grandson James said he also saw the girl's ghost."

The old woman frowned. "Whatever upset Alice must have also fooled him. I'm sure they saw something but I know it wasn't the ghost of Madeline Renais."

"Why not?"

"Because as Juliet pointed out the girl isn't dead. At least not to the best of our knowledge. It has to be all imagination."

"I hope so," she said, allowing a note of doubt to sound in her words. "Is there anything else I can do for you?"

"No," the old woman said. "I'll be fortunate if I'm able to sleep again after all this."

Madeline said goodnight and then returned to her own room. Not until then did she allow herself any feelings of exultation. She was delighted with the impact her ghostly appearance had made on the family. She only regretted that Raymond hadn't been there to register his reaction as well.

She was intrigued as to what it might have been.

The venomous glance which Thomas Copeland had offered her just before she'd wheeled his mother from the room convinced her that he suspected it was she who had appeared as the ghost. But he could not be sure. So he had to be tortured a little by the possibility that his son and daughter-in-law had seen a real ghost. And the strain had shown on him. At least she had made a beginning.

She slept lightly and several times wakened in the night thinking she'd heard the door to her room creak open. But these proved to be false alarms and she survived the night without any misadventure.

In the morning she found the weather changed. The sunlight had vanished and there was a thick fog, a gray mist such as she had never seen before. In conversation with Martha Copeland as they had breakfast together the old woman informed her it was a phenomenon which she could expect fairly often.

"The island is plagued with fog," the old woman declared. "And even on this hill above Dark Harbor it comes in thick."

"Will it last long?"

"It usually lasts for twenty-four hours or more," the old woman told her. "So you'd better resign yourself to it."

Martha made no mention of the ghost at breakfast. But after Madeline left her and went out to the front of the house, she came face to face with Raymond. He was wearing a sweater and dark trousers and he showed signs of excitement.

"Did you hear about the goings-on last night?" he asked.

She smiled wanly. "I suppose I was part of them. Your grandmother heard the fuss and insisted on my bringing her out here."

"And Ann and I slept through it," he said with some amazement. "What do you think about it?"

She looked at him very directly. "Let me ask you first."

The handsome man frowned. "I'd say Alice had some sort of crazy spell. Madeline Renais jilted me and ran off somewhere, but I have never heard of her being dead."

"Of course she could be dead without your knowing it," she said pointedly.

A strange look came to his face. "I suppose that is so."

"It's a possibility you have to consider."

He said, "And in that case?"

She shrugged. "I'd say in that case Alice might truly have seen a ghost. And James claims he saw it as well."

Raymond frowned. "There are no such things as ghosts."

"Too bad you can't convince those other two of that," she said lightly, watching his reactions carefully.

He said, "My father is very upset about it. He intended to return to Boston today, but between the fog and what happened last night he's decided to remain here."

"I suppose the fog makes the ferry crossing hazardous," she said.

"They don't make crossings on a day like this," he told her. "How do you plan to occupy yourself this morning?"

"I'll see your grandmother is comfortable and then I'll take a stroll," she said.

"In this damp fog?"

"Why not?" she asked. "It ought to be an experience."

"Don't expect it to be a pleasant one," he warned her.

She did exactly what she told him. She went to Martha's room and saw that she was having a morning sleep. Then she put on a cloak and overshoes and went out to stroll in the gardens. It was wet but not cold. She rather enjoyed the vista of the trees and landscape wreathed in fog.

It seemed to her that she'd had a major success in her ghostly appearance. And this was only a beginning. She must follow it up with another carefully planned move.

She walked in the fog for about a half-hour and then came back to enter the house. She was just a few feet from the rear door when she suddenly heard a sharp cracking noise from high above her. This was followed by a loud metallic thud, and she plunged toward the door fearful of what the sounds might mean.

CHAPTER NINE

Madeline stumbled against the door with a cry of terror as a giant mass of twisted metal came hurtling down within a few inches of her to crash on the ground. The shock of her near meeting with death left her pressed against the door and trembling. She stared at the weird conglomeration of iron, still dazed by it all.

Jethro the handyman came running towards her and asked, "You all right, Miss?"

"Yes," she said weakly.

He turned from her to gaze at the twisted metal with an air of disgust. "I told Mister Thomas the weather vane was in a dangerous condition. And I asked him to have the proper iron pipe sent over from the mainland to repair it, but he didn't do it."

"The weather vane?"

"You must have seen it up there," he said. "It was a good one, but the support weakened. He wouldn't listen to me and you were almost killed as a result. And the weather vane is ruined." He stared down at it grimly.

She was beginning to come around from her stunned state. She said, "But why did it come down just as I walked under it? Why wouldn't it happen in a windstorm or some time like that?"

The man with the red goatee eyed her with surprise. "You have a point there, Miss. I never thought of it being any danger on a day like this when it's calm. I could see it coming down when there was a blizzard or a hurricane!"

"No wind at all," she repeated.

The handyman frowned. "I'll go up there and take a look around, Miss."

"I wish you would," she told him. "And let me know what you find."

He nodded sagely. "I'll do that, Miss. First I'll get this mess out of the way before anyone stumbles over it."

She went inside leaving him to clean up the broken weather vane and then to try and see why it had so suddenly fallen. She thought she knew without having to go up there. She saw it as a direct answer to her ghostly appearance of the night before. Whoever knew her true identity had tried to do away with her in this fashion. It was only a miracle that she hadn't been instantly killed.

She was still trembling when she went into Martha Copeland's room. And to heighten her panic she saw that Thomas Copeland was standing by his mother's bed. Not only did she blame him for the original attack on her, but she believed that it was he who had sent the weather vane crashing down in an attempt to eliminate her.

The old woman in bed gazed at her with some concern. "You look ill," she said.

She said, "I've just had a narrow escape."

Thomas Copeland's face showed a strangely satisfied look. Very calmly he said, "Really? An escape from what?"

"The weather vane crashed down from the roof. It almost struck me," she said.

"You would have been killed!" Martha exclaimed.

"Yes, I would have," she said.

"The weather vane," Thomas said. "I seem to remember that Jethro told me it wasn't safe. I'd ordered a new pole for it but apparently it hasn't arrived."

"Apparently not," she said grimly.

Thomas still had that mocking air about him. He said, "At least we can be thankful you weren't hurt."

She looked hard at him. "What puzzles me is why it should fall when there isn't a breath of wind."

"That is strange," the old woman agreed.

The face of her son showed its usual glacier-calm. He said, "I wouldn't think there would have to be a wind. It had been ready to fall for some time and the moment came."

"Just when I was under it," she said.

"An unfortunate coincidence," Thomas Copeland said icily.

"I think so," she replied with as much sarcasm as she dared. She felt it was a duel of wills between them. She was trying to make him confess that he'd been her would-be murderer and was now trying to complete the grisly task.

"Let us be thankful that you're safe," the old woman said.

Thomas nodded. "You look as shocked as Alice was last night. One would think you'd also seen a ghost."

Martha Copeland snapped. "Don't bring up that nonsense again!"

Her son gave her a look of mild reproach. "You don't know how sure Alice is that she saw this ghost. It is quite amazing."

Martha said, "She is stupid as well as being too fat. I don't know what James ever saw in her."

"Alice comes from an excellent family and she will one day inherit a sizable fortune," Thomas Copeland said suavely. "I imagine James considers that perfection enough."

Martha's ancient face showed annoyance. "None of my grandchildren seems to have done well at selecting mates. Raymond allowed that nice French girl to get away from him."

"She wasn't a favorite with all of us even though you happened to like her," Thomas said with an icy smile as he glanced at Madeline.

His mother took no notice of this but went on, "And now it seems that Juliet is going to dally until Hudson Strout decides the engagement is hopeless and turns to someone else."

Thomas said, "I'll leave you to complain to Miss Ryan. I'm sure she'll be a much more sympathetic listener than I am." And with a bow he left the room.

The old woman grimaced. "Thomas can't bear to have me criticize him or any of his children. It's too bad his wife died so young. She was a good influence on him and would have helped the children. With her death he gradually grew more cold, and I'm afraid my grandchildren have suffered as a result."

"That could be," she agreed.

Martha glanced up at her. "You still look pale!"

"I did get a bad shock."

"Of course you did!"

Then she asked, "How long had your son been here before I arrived?" This was important. If he'd been with her a long while it eliminated him as a suspect.

The old woman said, "He just entered the room a moment before you. He was telling me about Alice and that ghost business when you came in."

"I see," she said tautly. So her suspicions had been well-founded and it was likely Thomas Copeland had sent the weather vane crashing down on her. Then he'd hurried to his mother's room to provide himself with an alibi.

Martha Copeland hunched against the pillows. "On this dark, foggy day I think I'll remain in bed. The dampness gets into my joints and makes them ache."

"Just as you like," Madeline said.

"Build a good fire in the fireplace and bring me some books," the old woman said. "I may as well make myself as comfortable as possible."

She did what the old woman asked and when the fire was blazing and Martha Copeland was deeply engrossed in a Dickens' novel, Madeline left the room. Making her way down the hall to the rear door she looked out and saw that Jethro had removed the mangled pieces of iron.

She was standing in the doorway when the handyman appeared from the direction of the stables. Seeing her he quickened his step and came up to her with a troubled expression on his face.

Jethro said, "I took a look on the roof, Miss."

"And?"

He hesitated. "I hate to say it, Miss, but I think there had been someone up there this morning. The door was ajar and I saw what might have been the mark of footsteps on the damp of the roof."

"Could you be sure of that?" she asked.

"No," he answered. "But I looked at the pole that bore the weather vane and I'd say some force had been applied to break it off. There are marks on it that look strange."

Madeline said, "But could you prove it?"

He shook his head. "No, Miss. But I don't like it. And I'd be careful if I were you."

"I'm sure that's excellent advice," she said. "Thank you, Jethro."

"Yes, Miss," he said. And he went on his way.

She returned to the house and her room. She no longer had any doubts that someone knew she was Madeline Renais and was trying to destroy her. In all probability it was the same person who had attempted to kill her in Brookline. All suspicion pointed to Thomas Copeland.

155

Would she be well-advised to find some excuse for giving up her post and leaving the mansion on Pirate Island? It might insure her safety but it would mean abandoning any hope of revenge or of straightening out things with Raymond. But was this important to her anymore? She must admit that it still was. And there was the danger to Ann Gresham. The girl should be warned.

Madeline felt she'd erred in not already having had a serious talk with the British girl. So far Ann had repulsed every attempt to help her and she hardly knew how to approach the girl to warn her what she might be facing. It was apparent that she'd have to risk being snubbed and try talking to Ann once again.

She returned to Martha Copeland and had lunch with her. The old woman was in a talking mood and lingered over her coffee chatting about the island and its people.

"We have a famous actors' colony not far from here," the old woman said. "I've often been at the Dark Harbor wharf and seen a handsome figure of a man with graying hair, arrayed in white flannels, wearing a scarlet geranium in his buttonhole, a tie to match the flower and a white silk band on his Panama hat. His name is DeWolf Hopper and he is a famous musical comedy star."

"I've read about him," she agreed.

Martha smiled. "He is a great prankster and a close friend of the beautiful Lillian Russell. When she visits the island, she always gets a warm reception from her friends. Before I broke my hip, I attended a party given in her honor."

"That must have been wonderful!"

"It was," the old woman said. "Raymond acted as my escort. Thomas never goes to such parties. But I knew I could count on Raymond." She paused to sigh. "So many changes since then. I'm a broken old crock and Raymond is no longer to be depended on."

She was struck by the sadness in the old woman's tone as she said this. "Do you mean that his health has become worse?"

Martha's sharp eyes fixed on her worriedly. "He has never really recovered from that illness he had. And he will not take care of himself properly. Perhaps if he married and settled down it might be different."

"He may marry this Miss Gresham," she suggested.

"Never!" Martha said. "Thomas will not allow it, for one. And none of the others like her."

"Can that possibly make so much difference? Won't Raymond have to make the final decision?"

"Raymond cannot stand up to the family when they unite against him," the old woman said.

"I suppose not," she answered, knowing from her own bitter experience that this was all too true.

The old woman went on reminiscing and Madeline lingered to listen. Then, wearied by her long talk and the heat of the fire, Martha Copeland lay down to have her afternoon sleep. This gave Madeline the opportunity she'd been seeking to have some time to herself.

She quietly left the room and went to the front of the mansion. She saw Juliet in the living room talking to her brother James. By the quiet, earnest tone of their conversation she judged they were discussing something important. Not wanting to intrude on them, she went upstairs and on impulse she ventured to the attic and the steps leading to the roof.

Opening the door to the roof, she stepped out into the fog-ridden air which made it impossible to see any distance. Down below she could see treetops emerging from the mist, but the view of Dark Harbor was completely obscured.

She ventured across the roof to the point where the weather vane had been standing. She saw the broken staff and the marks on the metal which looked like deep gouges. Jethro was right—someone had tampered with the pole and sent the weather vane plunging down towards her.

She was still examining the pole when she had the sensation of being watched. She had known these moments before and never had her instincts deceived her. Aware of her precarious position on the roof with only a low iron balustrade standing between her and the edge of the building she was overwhelmed by a chilling fear.

Slowly turning around she found herself face to face with the grim Thomas Copeland.

He said, "Why have you come up here, Miss Ryan?"

Feeling she was in desperate danger she struggled to be calm. How easy it would be for him to clamp a hand over her mouth to still her screams and shove her over the railing to her death. It would be no problem for him to get away safely before the incident was discovered and to disclaim any knowledge of what happened.

She said, "I was curious about the weather vane falling and I asked Jethro the way up here." She hoped this might stop him from attempting any violence. He would know that Jethro had discussed it all with her.

There was a cold glitter in his eyes. He said, "Curious about the weather vane, Miss Ryan? Why are you curious?"

"I'm still puzzled that it should collapse on such a calm day without a breeze stirring," she said, pretending to be more assured than she was.

"Accidents of the sort happen," he said evenly.

"Yes, you said that before," she agreed. She wondered if she dared start for the door to go back downstairs or whether any move on her part might trigger him to violence.

"It's cold and wet out here," he said. "Aren't you at all uncomfortable?"

"A little," she said.

His gaze was stern. "You puzzle me, Miss Ryan. I have the feeling you are not happy here."

"Oh?"

"Yes. It strikes me that perhaps I made an error in hiring you. Or at least James did. I believe it was he whom you first talked to."

"It was." She waited tensely, wondering what he might be leading to.

"Wouldn't it be better if you resigned your post here? I plan to go to Boston tomorrow. I could see you safely there."

She hesitated. "Let me think about it," she said. "If I should decide to accept your offer, I'll let you know tonight."

"I'd think about it seriously, Miss Ryan," he said. "We wouldn't want anything to happen to you."

Madeline knew it was an implied threat. But she did not care. Nor did she mean to let him bully her into leaving the island. She was certain that once she left the British girl would have some dreadful accident. The family hesitated to go ahead with whatever plan they had while she was still present.

She said, "Thank you for your thoughtfulness. Now I must go back down. I told your mother I wouldn't be up here long."

A strange look crossed his face. He said, "You told my mother you were coming up here?"

"Yes, she mentioned that the view was interesting when it was fine but she didn't think I'd see much in the fog. She was right."

Dull defeat showed in his cold eyes. He stood aside,

saying, "You shouldn't tarry up here or you're liable to catch a bad cold."

"That is true," she agreed, as she hurried past him, her heart pounding. Not until she was on her way down the stairs did she feel at all safe. It had been a nasty encounter and she was badly shaken.

When she reached the second floor landing, she saw Raymond in the reception hall below. He was arguing with his brother James and swaying drunkenly as his voice grew louder. James made some sharp statement and Raymond pushed him roughly aside, opened the front door and staggered out, slamming the door behind him.

Madeline felt this might be her ideal opportunity to warn Ann Gresham of her precarious position. She made her way along the dark corridor until she came to Ann's room at the rear of the house. She knocked gently on the door and Ann called her to come in.

She entered, closing the door after her. Ann was standing and staring out the window. She turned to Madeline with an expression of surprise on her attractive face.

"Yes?" Ann questioned her.

"Forgive my intruding," she said. "I felt I must speak to you."

"Speak to me about what?" Ann Gresham asked, taking a step towards her.

Madeline hardly knew how to begin. Her efforts to reach the British girl before had been notably unsuccessful. She said, "I think you should know that your life may be in danger."

Ann's eyebrows arched. "What a strange statement!"

"It's true," she insisted. "I know!"

"How could you possibly know?"

She said, "I've heard stories. There was another girl who

was to marry Raymond. He took her to his home in Brookline, and she vanished suddenly."

"I know about that!" Ann said. "She left of her own accord. She decided she didn't want to marry Raymond."

"I've heard a different version—that something happened to her. She had a serious accident as a result of the family's opposition to her."

"I don't believe it!" Ann protested.

"You would do well to," she told her. "The family is no fonder of you than they were of that other girl."

Ann eyed her indignantly. "Why do you mix yourself in this? You're little better than a servant here. How dare you come and tell me what I should do?"

"I only want to help you."

"That's ridiculous talk! I need no help from you," the other girl told her. "I think you have your eye on Raymond yourself and that is why you're trying to frighten me."

"You are wrong," Madeline said. "If you are wise you'll leave here as soon as you can," she said. "Get Raymond to go with you. But don't stay here with his family."

"I must stay here," the British girl said. "I need to win his family over."

"You'll never do that. They hate you!"

"How dare you say such things?"

"All I've told you is true," Madeline said urgently. "There is someone with murderous instincts among his family. I can't tell you with any certainty which one, but if you remain here long enough you'll be attacked. Probably murdered!"

"I will not have you trying to scare me this way," Ann Gresham said.

Madeline sighed. "I'll say no more. I won't bother you again. I only hope you'll listen to me."

"Why should I?" Ann demanded. "I think you must be more than a little mad."

Madeline felt depressed by the exchange. She turned to leave. With her hand on the doorknob she paused to glance over her shoulder and say, "One thing. Please don't tell the others that I was here and warned you."

Ann eyed her angrily. "Why shouldn't I? They ought to know how you've been bothering me!"

"I'm saying this for your own good," she said. "It will be best for both you and I if you make no mention of my visit." And she went out and closed the door without waiting for a reply.

She made her way downstairs with the feeling of failure. She was almost certain that Ann wouldn't listen to her and that she might complain to Raymond or the others about her. If she decided to do this it was hard to say what would happen.

A soft rain began to fall and this cleared some of the fog away. Madeline had dinner with Martha Copeland and then helped prepare her for the night. After taking care of these tasks she went to her own room. It had been a wearying day of complicated happenings.

She sat in a chair by one of the windows and listened to the rain. It was coming down more heavily and there was a light wind with it. By tomorrow morning the fog would probably have cleared and Thomas Copeland would be leaving Dark Harbor for his bank in Boston. She was to accompany him if she decided to give up her job.

These thoughts were running through her mind when she heard a soft knocking on her door. She opened it and saw that Raymond's father was standing there.

"Did you make up your mind about tomorrow?" Thomas Copeland inquired. "Are you going to remain on here or give up your post and journey to Boston with me?"

"I have decided to remain," she said quietly.

Anger showed on his gaunt face. "I'd say you were foolish!"

"Perhaps."

"You undoubtedly would be happier there."

"That may be true but I'm devoted to your mother. I think she needs me."

"I see," the gray-haired man jeered. "Well, let us argue about it no more. I can't see us agreeing."

"Nor can I," she said.

He bowed and went off down the corridor leaving her with the feeling that he had now come to a decision, that in a real way she had sealed her own doom by insisting on remaining.

The rain and fresh feelings of fear combined to bring her to the edge of despair. She sat before the last embers of the log fire and worried that she might have been foolhardy. Her plans for revenge wouldn't amount to much if Thomas Copeland found a means to end her life. A means which couldn't be traced to him and would seem accidental.

Yet she had an inner integrity, perhaps developed in her long struggle for recognition on the stage in her native France, which made her unwilling to back down from a stand once taken. And she did not want to retreat before the ominous threat of the Copelands. She wished that Sam Elder were there to counsel her, but he was more than a hundred miles away in Boston.

Hudson Strout could also be a tower of strength for her. But he had not yet shown himself. Probably he'd been delayed by the fog. She could only hope that he would arrive on the island within the next few days.

Wearied by it all she prepared for bed. And in spite of her fears she sank almost at once into a deep sleep. It was prob-

ably hours later, long after midnight, when she stirred rest-
lessly and in a kind of half-sleep felt sure she heard the door of
her room creak open.

As soon as this thought telegraphed through to her brain
she sat up in bed. Terror flared to a new peak when she saw
that the door of her room *was* open!

"Who is there?" she cried.

She trembled as she waited for an answer, almost knowing
there would be none. Whoever her phantom intruder might
be, it was unlikely he would identify himself. After waiting for
what seemed like hours, she threw back the bedclothes and
swung out of bed. She felt safer on her feet, ready for whatever attack might come from the blackness.

"Who is it?" she cried again.

And as she finished speaking, she saw a hooded black
figure move towards the doorway and vanish. It happened so
swiftly she thought at first it might have been an illusion. But,
no. Someone or something had been in the room!

Fighting her trembling she found a match and lit the
candle on her bedside table. Then by its wavering light she
moved slowly towards the open door. She went as far as the
doorway and stared out cautiously. The hallway seemed empty.

From the room across the way Martha Copeland called
out petulantly. "Mary! Mary, is that you?"

The sound of the old woman's voice calmed her nerves
and she crossed the hall into the other room. In the bedroom
she found Martha awake and upset.

"I heard screams!" the old woman complained. "What did
they mean?"

"I woke up and found my door open," she said, standing
by the invalid's bedside with the candle in her hand.

Martha gazed up at her with a frown on her thin face.
"And so you screamed?"

"I couldn't understand the door being open," she said. And then after a pause. "I also thought I saw a figure—a figure with a black hood. It moved across the room and then vanished."

"The ghost!" the old woman exclaimed.

"Ghost?"

"Yes," Martha said. "You must have heard the story of the hooded pirate who killed his henchmen. It is supposed to have happened here on this very spot. And the hooded ghost is said to haunt this house!"

"I've heard the story," she said, recalling that Thomas Copeland had told her about the phantom. Probably for the very good reason of covering up his own predatory moves against her.

"And you've taken it too seriously," the old woman accused her. "You've let it upset your nerves."

"No," she protested. "This was real enough. The door was opened!"

"You might not have closed it tightly and it swung open on its own. I've often known that to happen in old houses like this."

"I don't think that is the explanation," she said unhappily.

Martha Copeland's ancient face showed weariness. "I think the best thing you can do is go to bed and forget all about it."

"I'll try," she said.

"And don't start screaming again and waking everyone up," the old woman said. "Count to ten before you decide to panic and you'll find that you'll rarely reach the hysterical state."

She said goodnight to the old woman and went back to her own bedroom feeling humiliation and frustration. She might have known that Martha Copeland would be skeptical of her story. Perhaps for a reason. It could be that Martha knew that her son Thomas played the role of ghost when it suited him.

She placed the lighted candle on her bedside table and left it burning as she got into bed again. Last night she had played the role of ghost and accomplished some results. Tonight the tables were turned on her. Her nemesis in the Brookline mansion was giving her a taste of her own medicine.

She lay awake for a long while listening to the rain which was still coming down hard. Then her eyes closed and she fell asleep. This time she was tormented by nightmares in which the black-hooded phantom played a prominent role. She twisted and moaned through the ordeal of these fantastic and terrifying dreams.

Then she was roused by the sound of a voice screaming in the distance. She came awake with a start this time and listened for some sound besides the rain to come again to break the silence of the old mansion. And come again it did!

"Fire!"

There was no mistaking the word that was being screamed and she was suddenly flooded by panic. Fire in an ancient house such as this one could be a thing of terrifying swiftness. She had seen great tongues of flame destroy such a house in Boston within an hour.

"Fire!"

The cry came again as if someone were running through the corridors screaming it. She was now on her feet with her robe flung over her shoulders. Her first thought was of the old woman in the opposite room. She threw open her door and hurried into Martha Copeland's suite.

This time the old woman was sitting up in bed. In a trembling voice she said, "I heard someone call out fire!"

Before Martha finished speaking, there were more cries

and sounds of confusion and running footsteps from above. The entire household seemed to be coming awake. There were muffled voices from the servants' quarters and Madeline was sure that she smelled smoke.

She put down her candle and went to the old woman. "You must get out of bed and into your chair," she said briskly. "And put on something warm."

"Let us find out what it is all about!" Martha Copeland cried nervously.

"Not until we have you mobile and warmly clad," Madeline told her. "We may have to leave the house in a hurry!"

"No!" Martha moaned. "Not this house! It's the last link I have with my late husband. I can't lose this house!" She began to weep, making it even harder to get her into the wheelchair and bundled in a heavy coat.

There were people running down the corridor outside the room. And now a frightened-looking James poked his head in the bedroom doorway. He took in the situation and said, "You are awake! Good!" And he vanished.

"He told us nothing! The idiot!" old Martha Copeland said, caught between tears and anger.

"We'll find out soon enough," Madeline said as she began wheeling her out of the room.

"Go to the front of the house," the old woman ordered her.

She wasn't sure that this was wise but decided to obey her anyway. She started down the corridor and heard shouts in the front hallway.

They reached the reception hall and found the front door open and hastily-clad men standing at intervals passing up buckets of water. The line extended all the way up the stairs.

Juliet suddenly emerged from the confusion of faces and

people and came over to them. She said, "I think they'll be able to control it."

"Where is the fire?" Madeline asked her.

The blonde girl's face wore a strange look as she said, "In Ann Gresham's room."

CHAPTER TEN

Juliet's words came as another shock for Madeline. In the panic of getting the old woman safely in her chair and prepared to leave the house there hadn't been time to think about the cause of the fire. And now it seemed all too evident!

In Ann Gresham's room! Madeline realized bitterly that the British girl had neglected to heed her warning and had stayed in the old house too long. At the moment there was no telling what horror had overtaken her. Probably she was dead!

"In Ann Gresham's room?" Martha Copeland cried. "How did it start?"

"I don't know," Juliet said with a shrug and moved away.

The men were still in a frenzy, shouting and passing buckets. Now the smell of smoke was strong and curling smoke could be seen on the landing above.

Martha Copeland's face was peaked. "In Ann's room! I don't understand it!"

Madeline had to bite her tongue to prevent herself telling the old woman that she felt she understood only too well. She remained by the wheelchair ready to move her charge at a moment's notice. On the hopeful side the smoke did not seem to be increasing. Perhaps the fire would not be too bad after all.

In fact she began to expect this would be the case. The fire would be just large enough to cause Ann horrible burns or death, but contained to her room. Thomas Copeland would have surely taken care of that. And in her mind she was once again naming the gaunt-faced man as the culprit.

Suddenly, there was a shout from above and the bucket brigade halted its efforts as Thomas Copeland appeared on the landing.

"The fire is out," he called down. "All danger is over."

There were loud-voiced comments of relief. The men filed down the stairway and out the front door. Thomas Copeland came down to stand by his mother's wheelchair.

He said, "I'm sending Jethro for the doctor. Ann Gresham is alive but terribly burned. We've moved her to one of the guest rooms."

"How did the fire start?" the old woman wanted to know.

Thomas Copeland's face showed no expression. "It is difficult to say," he told her. "Apparently an overturned lamp. She must have gotten up in the night and lighted a lamp and then she must have stumbled. We found the room aflame and Ann unconscious on the floor close to the blaze. By the time we rescued her she'd suffered major burns."

"Dreadful! What about Raymond?" she asked.

"Not here," Thomas said in a grim voice. "He left for Kimble's Tavern early in the evening and he didn't come back. I'll have Jethro go look for him while he is in Dark Harbor fetching the doctor."

Martha's face was lined with distress. "Who is taking care of that unfortunate creature until the doctor arrives?"

"Juliet and the housekeeper," Thomas said. "Alice is still in shock from last night and James is useless in a crisis." Having delivered himself of this, the gaunt Thomas strode out the open front door.

"You can smell smoke strongly now," the old woman complained. "How could that girl be so careless?"

Madeline wanted to say that she didn't believe it had been a matter of carelessness. That she was almost certain the fire had been set by someone else and the British girl made to seem the culprit. Instead she confined herself to commenting, "If she was responsible for the fire, she has suffered the worst for it."

"Of course she was responsible," Martha said irritably. "You heard Thomas say so just now."

"That was his theory."

"The house could have burned down except for the quick action of the servants in forming that bucket brigade. They ought to be commended."

"I imagine either your son or some of your grandchildren will take care of that," she said.

"I'd expect so," the old woman said. "Now take me back to my room. All this fuss, and nothing came of it."

"You should be glad," she said, turning the wheelchair around and wheeling it back. Sometimes she found the old woman lacking in gratitude for her good fortune.

After a long moment of silence, the old woman said, "I think I would have died if we'd lost the house."

Madeline took her to her room and helped her back into bed. Then she returned to the corridor again and decided she would go upstairs to see how Ann was doing. The doorway of Ann's room was open and servants were already cleaning up the mess. Acrid smoke and the smell of things burned filled the air.

She saw James standing in the corridor by another door and at once assumed that the burned girl was in there. She went up to the thin, young man and saw that he looked pale and shaken.

"How is she?" she asked.

"Badly off," James said. "Juliet and the housekeeper are in there."

"Where is your wife?"

"In her room," James said bitterly. "The shock of the fire coming so soon after last night has prostrated her again."

She said politely, "It would be dreadfully disturbing."

"How is my grandmother?" James wanted to know.

"She has stood up the shock of the fire very well," she said. "I've just taken her back to bed."

James gave a deep sigh. "I wish the doctor would come."

"Yes," she agreed. She left him and went into the room where they'd taken Ann Gresham. Juliet and the elderly housekeeper stood whispering by the foot of the burned girl's bed. Madeline moved up to the bedside and was sickened by the sight of the girl's scorched hair and blistered face and arms. A thin sheet mercifully covered the rest of her body.

"She's in delirium," Juliet said.

"Not much wonder," Madeline answered.

She moved closer to the bed and the odor of burned flesh repulsed her. Just then the unfortunate Ann opened her eyes, stared dully at Madeline and then with great effort whispered something. Madeline at once bent close to hear.

"Black hood," the girl whispered. "Someone in a black hood!" And then she closed her eyes and seemingly lapsed into an unconscious state.

She moved away from the bed a little and Juliet followed her angrily. "Of course you won't pay any attention to what she said! That was all nonsense, that whispering!"

"I wonder," she said, staring at the other girl as the housekeeper stood uneasily in the background.

"You know it has to be nonsense," Juliet declared. "The girl is out of her mind!"

"She seemed quite rational to me for that moment," Madeline said. "It seems someone in a black hood came into the room and crashed that lighted lamp on the floor."

"Purely her imagination," Juliet argued. "Her mind rambled and went back to the ghost stories she's heard about this house. The stories about the ghost of that pirate in his black hood."

"You think that is the explanation?"

"It has to be!"

"I'm not that sure," she said.

Juliet began to look a little frightened. "What are you trying to say? That you believe a ghost started the fire?"

"No. That someone playing the role of a ghost did it."

"There's some excuse for her saying it in a delirium but none for you," Juliet snapped.

"Who raised the alarm that a fire had begun?"

Juliet hesitated. "I'm not sure. I think it was my father."

She thought grimly it would have had to be Thomas Copeland. Since he started the fire he would be bound to know about it first. She said, "It was lucky that he discovered it before it had spread too far."

"Yes," the blond girl agreed. "A little later on and it would not have been possible to save the house."

Madeline gazed at the bed again and saw that Ann Gresham was still unconscious. She felt a strong need to get away from the odor of burned flesh and quickly made for the door. James remained standing guard outside.

His face was chalk-white. He asked, "She's really bad, isn't she?"

"Yes," Madeline answered with irony. "I think you've been spared the ignominy of another undesirable sister-in-law."

"That is a cruel thing to say!" he declared.

"But I'm certain it is the truth," she said calmly and started down the stairs.

She went to her room. The rain had ended and as she gazed out the window she saw that it would soon be dawn.

She stretched out on the bed and managed to sleep a little. When she woke up it was daylight and there was sunshine again.

When the maid came with breakfast for Martha Copeland and her she brought the news that the doctor had arrived and was still up in the room with the severely burned girl attempting to save her life.

Sitting up in bed, Martha asked, "Do they think the chances are good?"

"No, Ma'am," the nervous maid said. "They think she will die."

After the maid left the old woman sipped at her coffee as she left the rest of her breakfast untouched. She said, "I don't feel like eating."

Staring at her own untouched tray of food Madeline agreed. "Neither do I."

"I wonder where Raymond is?" the old woman asked.

Madeline hesitated and then said, "According to his father he had gone to Kimble's Tavern, I believe. He hadn't come home at the time the fire was put out."

"Kimble's is an evil place. Raymond has spent far too many drunken nights there. You say that Thomas told you all this?"

"Yes. He sent Jethro for the doctor and also to find Raymond."

"Then he ought to be back by now. Of course he may not be in any kind of shape yet to realize what has happened," the old woman said bitterly. "I should think he'd feel guilt. He brought her here."

"I doubt that it was wise," she said quietly.

The old woman shot her a questioning glance. "And why do you say that?"

She said, "I think it was obvious that none of you welcomed her or considered her a suitable match for him."

Martha's lined face took on a guilty look. "Probably you are right. I didn't think it was so obvious. Give us credit, though, not one of us would have wished anything like this to happen."

One of you did! This was her thought, but she said, "I would hope not."

The door to the bedroom opened and Thomas Copeland came in. The strain of the night had told heavily on him. He came to the foot of his mother's bed and stood there as if in shock. He did not glance at Madeline.

Martha spoke up, "What is it, Thomas?"

He spoke dully, "The girl is dead."

Madeline gasped. So he'd managed the task successfully this time! He'd taken no chances. And what an actor he was, pretending shock and grief so convincingly. She felt like rushing up and pounding him with her fists.

The old woman said, "That is dreadful! What about Raymond?"

"He's back," Thomas said in the same dull voice.

"Is he badly upset about it?" Martha Copeland asked.

Her son shrugged with grim resignation. "I'm afraid I'm not able to tell much about my younger son. His process of thinking eludes me."

"He should never had brought that girl here in the first place," Martha said with a hint of irritation.

"I made that clear from the start," Thomas said.

"Now there will be a funeral and explanations and gossip, of course," the old woman went on bitterly. "This will be the second time that Raymond has been thwarted in marriage."

"I must go," the gaunt man said. "I have to look after the plans for the burial."

"Make it as hasty as is decently possible," the old woman said. "And find out from Raymond where her relatives are. They should be notified."

"Yes," Thomas said and went out.

Madeline found it hard to get away. Martha was upset by the news of Ann Gresham's death and so she fussed and fretted and demanded attention. At last Madeline made her comfortable and was able to leave. She at once walked down the corridor and out the rear door.

She crossed the lawn to the entrance of the stables and saw Jethro standing there talking solemnly to one of the grooms. He turned and saw her approaching and at once left the man to greet her.

"Good morning, Miss," he said, touching the visor of his cap. "Not that it can be that for anyone in this house."

"You are right," she agreed. "What a tragedy!"

"Yes, Miss," Jethro said soberly. "That Miss Gresham was a beautiful girl. Hard to believe what happened!"

"When you went to Dark Harbor last night did you locate Mr. Raymond?"

The face of the handyman registered disgust. "No, Miss. He had been at the Gray Heron, but by the time I reached there he'd moved on."

"So you didn't reach him to tell him the bad news?"

"No. He came back here later."

"I see," she said. "I wonder how he has reacted to the death of his fiancée?"

Jethro looked strange. "I tell you, Miss, you can't count on how the rich will act. They sometimes behave the opposite to what you and I would. I'd not be surprised if Mr. Raymond didn't show any grief at all."

"He must!" she protested.

"Don't count on it too much," the handyman warned her.

"You lost no time getting the bucket brigade organized," she commended him.

A pleased look crossed his plain face. "Mr. Thomas let us know about the fire and we had the buckets moving up there within five minutes of having the word."

"The fire didn't get beyond that one room."

"Went through the wall in one place," he said. "But that was all."

"You deserve credit," she said. "Were you one of the first in the room?"

"Yes, Miss. I was the one brought that poor girl out of the flames and smoke."

She was at once on the alert. She said, "Where was she when you found her?"

"On her side on the floor with the flames rising up to the left of her," he said.

"To the left of her?" she repeated in a surprised tone. "As I heard it she was crossing the room carrying a lighted lamp. She stumbled and the lamp fell and started the fire."

"That's the story, Miss," Jethro said.

"Then, wouldn't the lamp have been on her right rather than her left? I mean, she must have been carrying it in her right hand. It would be the normal thing to do."

Jethro looked bewildered. "That's true enough. And the fire would start where the lamp fell. Maybe she moved around it after she stumbled, trying to put the fire out after the lamp exploded."

She saw that a case could be made for this and that her suspicions would appear poorly founded. She said, "That could have happened."

She left him and strolled back to the garden area. On this fine summer day the gardens were a scene of colorful beauty. The atmosphere was pastoral and serene. She turned and gazed up at the fine old mansion. Who could guess that this impressive house was a breeding ground of evil?

How would she indict the Copelands for being the murderers they were? It would not be easy to convince others that this aristocratic family had banded together twice to break up unsuitable alliances between Raymond and young women of whom they did not approve. Both times the Copelands had planned murder. She had been fortunate enough to escape.

But had she been all that fortunate? Was not she twisted in both mind and body? Her face had been so altered that she'd been able to perpetrate this masquerade on them and her mind had been conditioned to the point where she was ready to commit murder if need be in revenge. The Copelands had truly left the mark of their wickedness on her!

And one of them knew her secret! That she was not the Maine girl Mary Ryan but the victim they had left to die in an alley at the height of a blizzard. Someone knew she was Madeline Renais! Attempts had been made to kill her. Thomas Copeland had also tried to frighten her away. And she had remained despite the dangers and threats.

Had she been wise? She wasn't sure of that now. Ann Gresham was dead. She'd failed in saving her. True the British girl had not given her any cooperation but she hadn't realized her danger. Madeline knew that as long as she remained in the old mansion her life was threatened, but she wouldn't leave. Not until she had let Raymond know the evil things his family had done to protect him from women below his station in life.

She was willing to accept that the Copelands really felt what they were doing was justified. Their moral code had become so muddled that they no longer were able to divide wrong from right. And it was her opinion that most of the family, probably with the exception of Raymond and old

Martha, knew what was going on. They might all be taking some part in the wickedness.

She had come to Dark Harbor full of plans to play her own ghost and terrify the guilty into revealing their guilt. Thus far she'd done no more than give Alice hysterics and frighten James. It was a pitifully small step in the masterful campaign she'd planned. Now this ugly murder, for she could think of it as nothing less, had transpired. Could she in the face of it go on with her plan?

She sank down on a wooden bench set out near some rose bushes and tried to sort it out in her mind. What to do? And what to do next!

"I've found you," it was a grim-sounding Raymond who spoke to her.

She looked up to see him standing before her. He gazed down at her with tormented eyes. She said, "I came out here to think."

"About what?"

"Many things."

"That's hardly an answer."

She grimaced. "About what happened last night. The shortness and tragedy of life generally."

"I've thought of that many times," he said.

She looked at him hard. "Yesterday at this time Ann was alive and well."

"I know," he said, his handsome face shadowed.

"You weren't here when it happened?"

"No." Guilt was prominent in his tone.

"In fact you were in town at Kimble's Tavern, probably drunk."

He said unhappily, "Why make drunkenness seem such a vice? I often drink to forget."

"Now you have something else to forget—Ann's death!"

He made a pained gesture. "You don't have to remind me of that."

"Are you really bothered that much?"

Raymond seemed startled. "How can you ask me that?"

"I just wondered."

"She was to be my wife."

She gave him a knowing glance. "And you brought her here knowing that your family was against the match."

"It was my right."

"But was it fair to her?"

He shrugged. "I don't know. Who can say? Her death was an accident. How can you blame it on anything but plain bad luck?"

She smiled bitterly. "That's an easy way out."

"Do you want me to blame myself?"

"If you think you should, yes."

"I don't know what to think," he said with a deep sigh.

"Because you aren't facing up to it," she rebuked him.

"You talk in riddles," he complained.

She got to her feet so she could better face him. She said, "I'm trying to make you understand that both times you've been engaged your family determined that you'd never marry the girls. And they went about making sure of it."

"That's ridiculous!" he protested. "For one thing it makes me seem incompetent to choose a proper wife."

Very calmly, she said, "I'm of the opinion they believe that."

"And you're hinting that they had something to do with Ann's death?" he said in a shocked voice.

"Yes," she agreed. "And with the disappearance of Madeline Renais. Or have you forgotten all about your other love?"

"No, I haven't forgotten about her."

"Well, then?"

180

"Madeline Renais left of her own accord. She simply walked out and never came back."

"And you didn't try to find out any of the circumstances?"

"No, if she thought that little of me, why should I?"

"I think I would."

He stared at her in silence. Then he said, "There's something about you. Every so often I get a kind of flash that you're not at all what you seem."

Nervously, she asked, "What do you mean by that?"

"You claim to be a naive young girl from Maine and yet you argue like a sophisticated woman of the world. It doesn't fit."

His words made a strong impact on her. She knew that she had almost betrayed herself before she was ready. She didn't want him to know who she was until she made at least one more attempt to uncover the murderer.

She hastily said, "I think you are confusing Maine common sense with sophistication. Perhaps they do resemble each other."

"I wonder," he said, his tormented eyes still fixed on her.

"What?"

He raised a hand wearily to his temple. "It doesn't matter. I feel as if my world had come down in ruins around me."

"You're too weak," she said. "You use drink too often as an escape!"

"Perhaps."

"You do!"

He turned away from her. "I don't know why the family is so particular about who is to be my wife. Probably both Ann and Madeline were too good for me!"

"Generous on your part," she said with sarcasm. "But I can promise you that your family doesn't share that feeling."

Raymond turned to her again, his face shadowed with

pain. "What do you want me to do? Go to them and challenge them with Ann's murder?"

"It would be interesting to see their reaction," she said. "Especially your father's!"

"I've caused him enough heartbreak already."

"So you refuse to take any stand? That's in character," she said. "I pity the next girl you show any romantic interest in."

He looked shocked. "Why do you say that?"

"She'd better be perfect. Otherwise she'll not last long. The family did so well this time, they'll not hesitate to strike again."

Raymond's handsome face wore a stunned expression. Slowly he said, "If I were to tell my father what you've just said he'd discharge you at once."

"I suppose he would," she agreed.

"Well?"

"I don't think you will tell him."

"Why not?" he asked.

"Because you have some fairness left though you are weak. Your grandmother is the only other one here I can trust. I think that both of you can be salvaged."

"And the others? My father, Juliet, Alice and James . . . ?"

"Are a cunning, bad lot."

"Prove it to me," he challenged her.

"Perhaps I will," she said. "Give me some more time."

"I said you were a strange girl," Raymond told her. "Now I think so more than ever, and I'll wait with interest for you to prove these things you've told me."

She looked up at him solemnly. "I think you are also in grave trouble. I wasn't able to save Ann. I'd like to try and save you."

"Mary!" he said her name with emotion and then he caught her by surprise as he took her in his arms and tenderly kissed her. It was a tense moment for her.

She pushed him away and said, "This is neither the time nor the place for you to do that!"

"I'm sorry," he said.

"You ought to be!"

He gazed at her long and hard. "But there was something about the instant when our lips met. It had almost a familiar ring."

"You're being stupid and imagining things!" she protested and hurriedly ran off so he would not see her blushing.

That afternoon the undertaker from Dark Harbor brought the plain, black coffin in which Ann Gresham was to be buried. The body was placed in it and the casket closed. It was then taken down to the big living room until the funeral the following morning.

Martha Copeland insisted that Madeline wheel her out to view the coffin. "I shan't be able to attend the funeral," she said. "So I'd like to see the coffin now."

When they reached the living room they discovered Thomas Copeland standing by the coffin with his head bowed and his hands clasped behind him.

His mother snapped, "Are you asleep, Thomas? Didn't you hear the creaking of my wheelchair?"

He slowly turned to her with a solemn look on his gaunt face. "It appears that I didn't," he said. "I was paying my respects to the corpse."

Martha eyed him grimly. "I'd say you have more respect for her in death than you did in life."

The gaunt man glanced at the closed coffin rather guiltily. "I wasn't aware of that."

"I think everybody else knows," his mother said. "Where is she to be buried?"

Thomas looked slightly embarrassed. He cleared his

throat. "In the family burial ground in Dark Harbor."

"I declare!" the old woman in the wheelchair said scathingly. "She wasn't good enough for us alive but she's being made welcome now that she's dead," his mother snapped.

He gave her an angry glance. "That's not a nice thing to say."

Martha declared, "But isn't it true?"

Her son went on, "The burial ground here has a Copeland lot which isn't much used. Most of the family is buried in Boston. There are a number of grave spaces available in the island lot. I think it practical and simpler to have the girl buried with those of the family resting here."

"So any of us could die here and be buried with her," Martha said. "How do you like that idea?"

The gaunt man looked uneasy. "I expect to be buried in our Boston lot."

"But you mightn't be," she warned him. "It could all depend on where you die."

"I don't think it worth arguing about," he protested.

Martha told him, "I'm very careful where I live and with whom I associate. In death, I would prefer to continue being choosy."

Thomas said, "Then you'd better stipulate in your will that you don't wish to be buried here!"

"I shall do that," she promised.

Madeline felt the entire conversation had taken a macabre turn. And it was in especially bad taste directly beside the coffin.

The grim atmosphere which Ann's tragic death had brought to the old mansion continued. Upstairs, workmen were already repairing the damage done by the fire. Madeline spent the day in her own room. She tried to read but paced nervously most of the time.

Thomas Copeland had postponed his trip to Boston until

after the funeral. She wondered why Hudson Strout hadn't shown up on the island yet. And she realized that Ann would be dead and buried before his arrival.

She knew that all her fears were gathering momentum in the brooding old mansion which seemed more ominous and threatening than ever.

With the coming of darkness she felt even more nervous. As she helped prepare Martha Copeland for the night, she clumsily let a candle holder fall.

The old woman stared at her. "I have never seen you do anything like that before!"

"I never have," she agreed as she retrieved the holder and candle from the carpet. "I'm nervous tonight."

"I can see that," Martha said, studying her sharply. "Surely you don't believe in ghosts."

"I'm no longer certain of it."

"Rubbish!" the old woman said. "I'm a good deal older than you and I have never seen one—at least not that I could prove. I have been scared by shadows."

Madeline gave her a knowing look. "But you are not really sure about those shadows, are you?"

"I won't say I believe in ghosts!" the old woman insisted.

She stayed with the invalid until she sank back on her pillow in sleep. Then she left and went across to her own room. It was an eerie night with the corpse of the mutilated Ann Gresham resting out there in the living room. Thomas Copeland seemed obsessed by the coffin, and she had a feeling that he might return to it when he decided everyone else had gone to bed.

The more she thought about this the more likely it seemed. And she began to plan. What more dramatic moment for her ghost to appear than beside the coffin of the woman whom Thomas had murdered? If ever there was a time to break down his resistance and have him admit his guilt, this must be it.

But against this she felt little like going through the theatrical performance of donning the robe, makeup and wig to become Madeline Renais. It seemed heartless to indulge in the masquerade with Ann lying there in that black coffin. And yet it was to avenge herself and Ann that she would go through the ordeal of playing ghost.

This might be the time when her enemy's defenses would be soft. She had noted the nervous apprehension in Thomas Copeland as he'd talked to his mother about the burial of the British girl in the family lot.

That decided her. She went over to the closet and stood on the wicker chair to reach the shelf where her disguise was hidden. For a frightening moment she thought it wasn't there. Then she found it.

CHAPTER ELEVEN

She carefully brought down the various items. As she sat before the dresser mirror to make up, she discovered she was trembling. Because her hands were not steady it took her longer than usual to perfect the disguise. She prayed that Thomas Copeland would not visit the coffin and leave before she went out there. At the same time she wryly questioned herself why she should so strongly believe that he would make that pilgrimage to the coffin in the dark.

Was there a voice from the other side whispering this to her? Was Ann's ghost urging her on to this impersonation? Was it possible that the girl who refused to cooperate with her in life was now insistent on helping her in death? These weird questions echoed through her troubled mind.

She touched the grease paint expertly to her nose to restore it to its former shape. Next she patted the wig in place and then stood up and donned the white robe with which she hoped to achieve a ghostly effect.

The moment had come for her to go and wait with the corpse to see if her theory might be right. She felt torn between going and staying in her room, but she realized that if she didn't go ahead now, it would be because of her own cowardice.

She extinguished the lamp on her dresser and left her room. Gliding down the hall in ghostly fashion she watched with bated breath to see if there might be anyone in the reception hall. There was no one.

She continued on and came to the double doorway leading

to the living room. In a corner at the front end of the room was the coffin. Moonlight shone in through a tall window and cast a beam of melancholy blue light on its shining surface.

After a moment she moved into the living room to stand in the shadows just beyond the moonlit coffin. She was on her way to this spot when all at once from the shadows in the middle of the room she saw a figure take shape and come towards her!

It was the black-hooded monster! And as she tensed with fear she knew she dare not scream. To do so would mean revealing herself as the ghost of Madeline Renais. The figure in the black hood lunged at her and she silently turned and fled from the room. The phantom was at her heels as she reached Martha Copeland's room, opened the door and rushed inside.

Slamming the door she pressed hard against it, trembling. At the same time the petulant voice of the old woman cried out, "Who is it?"

"It's only me, Mrs. Copeland," she said, her voice taut as she remained standing with her weight against the door.

"What are you doing roaming around at this hour?" the old woman wanted to know.

"I thought I heard someone in the corridor."

"You're much too jittery," Martha Copeland reprimanded her. "I didn't hear anything."

"It seems I was mistaken," she said, relaxing a little as it appeared the black-hooded figure wasn't attempting to follow her into the old woman's quarters. But dare she return to her own room?

Martha Copeland said, "Well, if you're going to stay here awhile, you might as well light a lamp!"

"No!" she said, almost revealing her panic in her frantic reply.

"Why not?"

Madeline knew if she put a lamp on and the old woman saw her in this disguise there would be a strong reaction. She had no idea what it might be, but she wasn't going to risk it.

She said, "I'm going back to my room now."

"You'll try and sleep and not have any more of these nervous spells?" the old woman asked.

"I'll try very hard," she promised. "Good night."

"Good night," the old woman grumbled. "No wonder people find it hard to sleep after all that has gone on here."

She hardly dared breathe. She opened and shut the door very quickly as if she'd gone out. But she didn't dare leave with the figure in the black hood, still lurking out there. She groped in the dark until she found an easy chair and then sank into it. She remained in the chair not making any sound to reveal her presence to the old woman. Finally she heard Martha sleeping and in a short time she fell asleep herself.

She awoke with a crick in her neck and saw the sun shining in through the window. Fortunately, Martha Copeland was still asleep. She rose stealthily and made her way to the door. Ever so gently she twisted the knob aware that any undue sound might at once waken the old woman and expose her in disguise.

She opened the door and tiptoed out, closing it after her. Then she raced across to her own room and went inside. She was not prepared for the sight which greeted her. Her room was a shambles. The figure in the black hood must have visited it in search of her and, not finding her there, had vented his wrath on the room. Everything was torn up and thrown about.

With a deep sigh she removed her makeup and costume. When she'd safely hidden the disguise away again, she began to straighten out her room. Every desk drawer had been opened and emptied. Things were scattered in a mad fashion.

She knew there was nothing she could do at this point but put things back in place.

She had barely finished before it was time to join Martha Copeland and help her start the day. She arrived in the old woman's room at the same time as the maid with the breakfast tray.

The maid explained, "I'm going to the funeral. So I'm doing my chores early."

"Don't regard me as a chore, young woman," Martha Copeland said sternly.

"No, Ma'am," the girl stammered and rushed out.

"You've frightened her," Madeline said, beginning to set out various dishes from the tray for the old woman's benefit. "She may never come back."

"Did you finish your night wandering?" Martha asked grumpily as she began to cut up a griddle cake.

"Yes, I'm sorry I woke you up."

"You should have thought of that first," was the reply. "I must say you sounded terrified."

"I was. Any noise in the night which I can't explain bothers me now. So many terrible things have happened."

The old woman occupied herself with her breakfast, halting between mouthfuls to make an occasional comment. She said, "We'll all feel better when that coffin is out of the house."

Madeline glanced up from her breakfast tray with an expression of surprise. "You can't be frightened of poor Ann Gresham's corpse."

Martha nodded. "Any dead body in the house bothers me. It has been awhile since we've had a funeral from here."

Madeline was forced to the conclusion that the old woman in her charge was almost as unfeeling as the others. She showed no sadness about Ann's death but simply wanted her body to be removed from the premises.

Madeline said, "The funeral is to be this morning so it won't be too long."

"Are you going?"

"Yes," she said. "I think I should."

"You didn't know her well."

"No one here did," she said. "But it seems a mark of respect I ought to show her."

They discussed the funeral no more. Madeline was depressed because she'd missed her opportunity to surprise Thomas Copeland the previous night. He'd seemingly turned the tables by coming out of the shadows at her in that black hood. Then he'd gone to her room to cause all that wanton damage.

Her attempt to play ghost had ended in near disaster. The next time she tried this game she'd have to be much more wary. But it was difficult to see everything in the midnight blackness. One thing was certain, the figure in the black hood was not afraid of the ghost of Madeline Renais. This meant that it would be impossible to shock Thomas Copeland into confessing.

As soon as breakfast was over she left the old woman to put on a black dress and a hat with a thin black veil for the funeral. When she was properly attired she went to the front of the house to join the others. She saw that everyone had turned up for the occasion. They were all standing in the living room not far from the coffin.

Thomas Copeland in long black coat and trousers was near the doorway in earnest conversation with the clergyman who was to conduct the funeral. Juliet was inside the living room standing with a dour Alice in black veil and dress and a pinched-looking James in a black suit. Raymond stood apart from the others with a solemn look on his handsome face.

When he saw her he came towards her.

"You're going to the funeral?" he said.

"Yes."

"That is very considerate of you."

"I want to attend."

"I don't," he said, his face shadowing.

"No?"

"No," he said. "The full impact of Ann being dead has just hit me. I don't feel equal to hearing the service and seeing her lowered in the ground."

She stared at him. "You must have planned to go to the cemetery, you're dressed for the occasion."

"I did intend to go. I changed my mind a few minutes ago."

Madeline said, "If you don't go it may cause talk."

He looked angry. "I don't care."

She noticed that his hands were shaking again and reminded herself that he was not well. Perhaps he was being wise in his strange determination not to go to the funeral.

She said, "I suppose you know what is best for you."

He licked his lips nervously. "I look at the coffin and I keep seeing her face—hearing her voice!"

She frowned. "You weren't like this yesterday!"

The handsome Raymond showed guilt. "I was too hung over from my night of drinking yesterday to really feel what had happened. Now it has come to me."

"So it seems," she said with mild disgust.

Thomas came over to them and said brusquely, "The carriages are ready. We will leave in a few minutes. The Reverend Davis is anxious to get on to the cemetery."

Raymond looked at him. "I'm not going."

The older man registered shock. "Not going?"

"No." Raymond's voice rose a little.

His father glanced around nervously to see if anyone had noticed and seeing that they hadn't, he spoke to his son with some intensity. "She was your fiancée. You brought her here. You have a duty to go!"

"Which I shall neglect as I've neglected so many others," the unhappy Raymond told him.

Thomas Copeland stood staring at him with that familiar coldness. "Very well," he said at last. "If that is your decision. The rest of us will get on with it." And he turned his back to his younger son to speak to the clergyman again.

Raymond gave her a forlorn look. "Don't think too badly of me," he said.

"I can't blame you for being sensitive to Ann's death," she admitted. "Though I do wish you felt like attending the service."

"I can't," he said. And he left her to go upstairs.

Juliet came out to join her and said, "I believe we are to be in the same carriage."

It was almost a half-hour before the slow procession reached the cemetery just beyond the town of Dark Harbor. It was a well-kept burial ground with many fine tombstones.

Cemetery laborers had opened a grave and stood respectfully in the background waiting to shovel back the earth after the service. The pallbearers included Thomas Copeland, James, the doctor and three of the male servants. Madeline thought it ironic that Thomas, who'd probably contrived the girl's death, should be the most prominent pallbearer.

In a way she could not blame Raymond for not wanting to attend the funeral, especially if he'd taken her words seriously and was beginning to suspect that the other members of his family were responsible for the British girl's tragic death. There was a hush among the assembled group as the clergyman began intoning over the coffin.

She had left the Copeland family and was standing a little distance from them near the servants who had attended the funeral. She was listening to the old clergyman and wondering what Raymond might be doing at home as the service went on.

Then someone came quietly up and stood at her side. A man's voice whispered, "I'll want to talk to you alone a little later."

She looked out of the corner of her eye and almost cried with relief at the sight of Hudson Strout standing there. The young lawyer had his hat in hand and looked somber in the black suit he'd worn for the occasion.

She whispered back, "I've been waiting for you."

"Delayed. Too bad about the Gresham girl."

"I did what I could," she whispered.

"I'm certain of that," he replied. "After the service I'll have to pay some attention to Juliet. But I'll see you in the gardens later."

"I'll be there," she promised.

The clergyman had ended his oration and the coffin was being lowered in the grave. The assembled company came into motion again, there were groupings in earnest conversation as the grave diggers waited with obvious impatience to begin their work.

Hudson Strout told her, "Remember what I said."

"I will," she promised.

He said, "Your disguise is perfect. I'd never think you were Madeline Renais. It's better than it was that day you fooled Sam and I."

"How is Sam?"

"Worried about you."

"I've thought of him," she said. And then in a taut voice

194

she added, "They're staring at us. Wondering how we know each other."

Hudson Strout said, "I'll tell them I looked after your aunt's legal affairs in wherever it was you're supposed to have lived."

"Just outside Portland, to the north!"

"I'll remember," he said and with a nod he left her to join a disgruntled Juliet. The blonde girl had been watching with annoyance.

James and Alice Copeland came over to Madeline. He said, "You are to go back in the carriage with Alice and me. Juliet wants to ride alone with Hudson Strout. They're engaged, you know."

"I think someone told me that," she said.

Alice gave her a suspicious look. "How do you happen to know him?"

"He was my aunt's lawyer," she said. "He came to look after her will before she died."

Alice's eyebrows lifted. "She couldn't have left you much or you wouldn't be working as a companion."

"My aunt had many other relatives," she said. "By the time her money was divided there was little for any of us."

James looked disinterested. He said, "We'd better hurry or the carriage will be leaving without us. I'm not ready to remain here just yet."

The ride back was dull and depressing. James and Alice sat looking sour and saying nothing. Madeline kept thinking about Raymond and feeling rather sorry for him. She was also glad that Hudson Strout had finally reached the island. Now she would have more courage in playing the ghost.

When they reached the house she went straight to Martha Copeland's bedroom. The old woman was in her wheelchair and full of curiosity.

"Tell me about the service," she said.

"It was rather long."

"It always is when that funny old clergyman officiates," Martha Copeland said dolefully.

"Hudson Strout is here. He joined us during the service."

"That lawyer," the old woman said. "Well, that ought to put Juliet in a better humor, though I doubt if he'll ever marry her."

"They are engaged."

"Because she wanted it," Martha said with a grim look. "I know she urged him into it. And as a result he has refused to name a wedding day."

"They came back together in one of the carriages."

"Would you believe it? Raymond came down here with me for a while," the old woman said. "I've never known him to be so upset."

"I saw that he was shaken. And he refused to go to the cemetery."

"I think he was wise," Martha said. "That girl's death has hit him hard."

Madeline smiled sadly. "He didn't seem to worry about the Renais girl nearly that much."

"She didn't die! She left him."

Madeline said, "She could be dead for all he knows."

The old woman stared at her. "Why do you say that?"

"He didn't try to find her. He knows she vanished and that is all."

Martha Copeland showed concern. "I was ill at the time. They thought I was going to die. I know little about it. But they told me she left in a temperamental rage."

"I wonder."

"You seem very interested in that girl," the old woman said.

Madeline blushed. "I'm simply curious as to why he showed so little feeling about his first loss."

"It wasn't a death," Martha insisted. "You must get that into your head. Ann's death was horrible and unexpected. But if I had to pick between her and Madeline Renais, I would pick that French actress any day. I told him so when he was down here mourning Ann."

"What did he say?"

"He admitted that he'd been deeply in love with Madeline, but he shut his heart to her when she left him."

"Which I think stupid."

The old woman shrugged. "Just a point of view, my girl. See if lunch is ready. I'm starving."

Madeline hurried the cook with lunch and then shared it with the old woman. Afterward, when Martha settled down for her afternoon nap, she had her first opportunity to go outside. She'd changed from black to a favorite fawn-colored outfit.

As she stepped outside, Nero came bounding up and nuzzled his head against her dress. She patted him and said, "How are you boy? I'd almost forgotten you!"

The Dalmatian lapped her hand and when she strolled in the direction of the garden he frolicked along at her side. Suddenly Thomas Copeland appeared from behind a hedge and confronted them. The dog at once stopped playing and began to growl at the gaunt man in black.

Top hat in hand, Thomas Copeland gave the big dog a scowl. "Nero does not have good manners," he said.

"I think you frightened him. You came on us so unexpectedly."

He gave her an annoyed glance as Nero remained standing there with his hackles raised. He said, "I don't expect to be reproved by a dog."

"I'm sure he means no harm," she apologized. And she

turned to Nero and in a soothing tone said, "Be a good boy and run off and play."

The black and white dog looked up at her for a moment and gradually relaxed, then ran off behind them. In a few seconds he was out of sight and she felt less tense.

Thomas Copeland's face was derisive. "You seem to have a charm over animals."

"I think speaking kindly to them works in most cases," she said.

"Perhaps," was his thin-lipped reply. His eyes fixed on hers. "I find it most interesting that you and Hudson Strout are friends."

"We happen to know each other," she said.

"Well, whatever!" the gaunt man said.

She was certain he had penetrated her disguise and that now he was even more suspicious because she knew Hudson Strout so well. She hoped it might restrain him from any immediate attack on her.

She added, "He wrote my aunt's will."

"I see," Thomas Copeland said with that steely glint in his eyes. "I wondered."

She asked, "When are you going to Boston?"

"Not until the first of the week," he said. "After the delay of yesterday I may as well wait for another week."

"Perhaps I'll go with you then," she said.

This did not seem to delight him. He said, "You can let me know later." It was almost as if he no longer wanted her to leave. This could well be because he'd decided she had to die. And it would be easier for him to get rid of her on the island.

He went on towards the house leaving her to stroll alone in the garden. More than ever she believed that Thomas Copeland was the murderer. She had an idea that the rest of the family rallied around him but that he was the master of evil among them.

She walked to the extreme edge of the gardens and then started back again. It was on her way back that she saw Hudson Strout hurrying to join her. The pleasant young lawyer came up to her in a rather breathless state.

"I've rushed all the way," he said. "I had a bad time getting away from Juliet."

She smiled wanly. "I thought you might have."

"The girl was actually jealous of you," he complained. "And we only exchanged a few words in the cemetery."

"I've found her touchy," Madeline said.

"Worse than that, she's bad-tempered," the young lawyer complained. "And all the time she was rambling on, I knew you were out here waiting for me!"

"Well, you're here at last," she said.

He nodded grimly. "Yes, let's go sit somewhere and talk."

She told him, "There's a bench over beyond that hedge."

"Good," he said taking her arm.

They strolled across to the bench and sat facing each other. She said, "No one comes here so we shouldn't have to worry."

He sighed. "I don't want to get you in any kind of trouble."

"I'm afraid I'm in trouble already."

"I've seen Raymond just now," he said. "He looks ill. I'd say he's lost a lot of weight since I last saw him."

"It's too bad," she agreed. "He drinks far too much and Ann's death has upset him."

"A horrible business," he said. "Tell me how it happened."

She gave him a detailed account and ended with her own suspicions. "I think Thomas Copeland started the fire and caused her death. He probably stunned her so she couldn't flee from the room."

The lawyer stared at her. "You seem to have no doubt he is the murderer."

"I haven't," she said. "I do think he's had assistance from James, Juliet and even from stupid, fat Alice. But I consider him to be the ringleader."

"He is cold. I can't deny that," Hudson Strout worried. "But a murderer?"

"No one else fits into the puzzle as neatly as he does," she said.

"What about your ghost impersonation? Have you tried it?"

"Twice."

"And?"

She sighed. "I wasn't eminently successful!"

"Tell me about it."

She did and finished by saying, "Now that you're here I'm going to play the ghost again."

He frowned. "Is there any point?"

"What do you mean?"

"If Thomas knows who you are, he isn't going to be bothered by your impersonating a ghost."

She said, "He wasn't when he came after me in the living room in that black hood the other night."

"So what is the point?"

"I want to find out how deeply the others are involved," she said. "And to what extent they should be punished. I tried it on Alice and she went into near hysteria."

Hudson Strout looked bleak. "So she must think Madeline Renais is dead."

"I'm sure she does. I think they all did until Thomas Copeland recognized me as Madeline in disguise."

The lawyer smiled. "I don't know how he did. You even sound like a Maine girl. You must have practiced a lot to perfect your performance."

She gave him a grim smile. "I always try to play any part to perfection."

"And now you're playing the most important role in all your life," he said earnestly.

"A murder drama with a real murderer," she said.

"Sam Elder is worried sick about you!"

"I wish I were back in my cottage," she said wistfully.

"You really do?"

"Yes, I'm beginning to realize how happy I was there. But I had to spoil it by getting this plan for revenge."

The young lawyer argued, "You couldn't remain in a cottage for the rest of your life shut away from the world."

"It wasn't so bad."

He smiled in amazement. "I can't believe I'm hearing this from the glamorous Madeline Renais."

She raised a finger to her lips. "It isn't wise to say that name."

"I'm sorry," he said. He glanced around. "The island is pleasant enough and Dark Harbor is a quaint little town; the only bad thing is the atmosphere of this place."

"The Copelands are a neurotic family," she said. "I have never before met a group quite like them. And I don't want to meet any such group again."

"I agree," Hudson Strout sighed. "What can I do to help?"

"Stay here as long as you can."

"I plan to remain the weekend," he said. He gave her an earnest look. "Now that Ann Gresham is dead, one thing bothers me more than anything else."

"What?"

He asked, "Are you still in love with Raymond?"

She hesitated. Then she said, "No, I'm afraid not."

The lawyer's face brightened. "Don't feel badly about it. I say it is the best of news."

"I hate to admit it," she said. "I loved him once. But

now I only feel sorry for him."

"Then why quarrel with your feelings?"

She made a frustrated gesture. "I can't understand the change. I can't blame him for not trying to find me. They lied to him and then quickly rushed him out of the country."

"But he let them do it," the young lawyer pointed out.

"He's weak."

"You must have known that for some time."

"Not as I do now," she said. "I allowed myself to be blinded by his charm. That's all over."

"Good," he said.

"And bad," she sighed. "One hates to be robbed of illusions. Especially when you've paid so highly for them. Because of my love for Raymond, I made myself a target for the Copelands."

"As Ann Gresham did later."

"Yes. I knew something dreadful would happen."

The young lawyer said, "I think if nothing is found out by the time the ferry leaves for the mainland on Monday morning you should join me in going back to Boston."

"Something is going to happen before then," she said solemnly.

"How can you be sure?"

"Because of the way Thomas Copeland behaved. I'm certain he will try to murder me before I can get away."

"Why? You're no longer interested in Raymond. He must guess that."

"He knows that I am convinced he is the murderer and he's probably afraid I have some sort of proof against him."

"That would make him desperate to silence you," Hudson Strout agreed.

"So we can only wait."

"You'll do more than that, I'm sure," he said.

"Yes," she agreed. "If I have the chance I'll play the ghost again. And maybe this time more success will crown my impersonation."

Hudson Strout glanced towards the house. "I intend to have a frank talk with Juliet before I leave."

"Oh?"

He nodded. "Yes. It's time I stopped playing my particular little game. I'm going to be honest and tell her that our engagement is a farce and we should never marry."

"She'll blame me!"

"She should."

Madeline gasped. "Why do you say that?"

"Because I've fallen hopelessly in love with you," he said with a burst of emotion. "Surely you must have known that for some time. I told you but I couldn't press you too far as long as you were in love with Raymond."

She gave him a worried look. "This could get very complicated," she warned him.

"I'm all for the direct attack," was his reply as he took her in his arms in a warm embrace.

She remained there for several long moments and when they parted, she sighed and said, "Haven't we enough problems without creating more?"

"It will be all right," he said. "I should have been frank with Juliet long ago. Now let's go back to the house."

They strolled back, lost in their thoughts, and saying little. She left him in the reception hall and went to Martha Copeland's apartment. She found the old woman seated in her wheelchair and fully awake.

As soon as she entered the room the old woman gave her a strange, penetrating look and said, "I've been thinking about what you said concerning Madeline Renais. And I have something important to tell you about her."

CHAPTER TWELVE

There was something slyly insinuating about Martha Copeland's manner and Madeline at once tensed. She tried to hide
her agitation as she asked, "What have you to tell me about
her?"

"I know where she is," the old woman said with relish as
she leaned forward in the wheelchair.

"You do?" she said in a faint voice.

"Yes."

"That's very interesting," she said nervously.

The old woman gave a harsh chuckle. "I think it is! Now
why don't you ask me to tell you where she is?"

She bit her lower lip. How should she handle this? It was a
bad setback just when she was ready to make the big effort to
find her would-be murderer.

She said quietly, "Very well, tell me. Where is she?"

Martha Copeland sat back in her chair. Then she said,
"Right here in this room."

"In this room?"

"Don't pretend, girl," the invalid snapped. "I'm not as old
or as foolish as you might wish to believe. I put two and two
together from what you said and I suddenly realized why all
along you have seemed so familiar to me. You are Madeline
Renais!"

She hesitated. "I could easily deny it."

"Why bother?"

"I haven't admitted anything."

"You don't have to."

"So you think I'm Madeline Renais. What are you going to do about it?"

"Not a thing!" the old lady declared.

She was startled. "Then why have you told me this?"

"Because I wanted to let you know you aren't deceiving me," Martha Copeland told her. "Behind those glasses and despite that bleached hair I see Madeline Renais."

"I'd rather not discuss it," she said.

"You needn't," the old woman told her. "I have always favored Madeline and I think things happened when I was ill of which I wouldn't approve. So I'm on her side."

"I'm sure she'd be grateful," Madeline said careful to keep up a thin line of pretense that she was not herself.

The old woman studied her with interest. "What I'm anxious to find out is why you came back in this weird disguise?"

"Why don't you just be patient," she suggested.

"I never was known for my patience," the old woman said. "I frankly am curious. What do you hope to accomplish here?"

She smiled bleakly. "I'm here as your companion."

"You hornswoggled my grandson into hiring you," the old woman chuckled. "I consider that a major victory when I recall how anxious they once were to get you out of the house."

Madeline faced the old woman soberly. "Whatever you may think I ask you to keep it to yourself for at least a few days. After that I'll be happy to discuss things with you."

"If that is what you wish," Martha sighed.

"Can I depend on you?"

"I gave you my word. It is rarely questioned. But I do wonder if Raymond knows about you. He has given me no hint of it if he does."

"That's another thing I can better answer later," she said.

"There is something different about your face aside from your disguise," the old woman said staring hard at her. "I think it is your nose. The conformation of your nose is not the same as it was."

Madeline changed the subject saying, "Is there anything I can do to make you comfortable?"

"Yes," Martha said. "Help me back into bed. I'm tired. And clear this mystery up as soon as possible. My nerves can't stand the suspense."

She transferred her charge to bed and Martha closed her eyes for a late afternoon nap. She went back to her own room and stared at her reflection in the mirror. The plain girl with spectacles and blond hair whom she saw was a stranger, and yet another person in the mansion had seen through her disguise.

She was glad that Martha Copeland had come out with her conviction that she knew her. She'd at least been warned. Could she depend on the old woman to keep the knowledge to herself? After some brief speculation, she decided that she could. Martha, though frail and old, had the strongest character of all the Copelands. And the old woman had made it clear she was on her side.

However, it seemed that the tensions were racing to a peak. She either had to succeed in routing out the killer this weekend or give up the project. It would be pointless and much too risky to hang on longer.

She went to the living room and was standing there alone when Juliet came into the room. The arrogant young woman was wearing a fancy yellow dress and broad-brimmed summer hat. She carried a parasol in her hand and she halted to give Madeline a patronizing look.

"I saw you from my window awhile ago," she said.

"Did you?" Madeline said cautiously.

"I understand you know Hudson from somewhere before," Juliet went on.

"Yes."

"Let me warn you that he is engaged to me," Juliet said icily. "I'll thank you for keeping away from him."

This annoyed Madeline and she flashed back, "He happens to be an old friend. I'll feel free to talk with him whenever I like!"

"Really?" was Juliet's cold comment. "I shall have something to say to Hudson about that. I will not be made ridiculous by you two!"

"If anyone is being ridiculous it is you!"

"We'll see about that," the other girl said and with a toss of her chin, she turned and left the room. A moment later the front door opened and closed as she went out.

Madeline remained in the living room shocked by Juliet's show of bad manners. She had always thought her difficult to get along with, but she was astonished that the girl should show her jealousy so openly.

Suddenly Madeline realized that she was standing in almost the exact spot where Ann's coffin had rested. This brought thoughts of the unfortunate British girl rushing to her mind. She recalled the jealousy Ann had shown of Raymond. She had not realized who her true enemies were. She had not learned to fear the Copelands!

She lingered a few minutes longer in the stifling atmosphere of the living room. The Copelands rarely opened a window and so the old mansion had a dank, aged odor. She decided that she must escape and quickly followed Juliet out the front door. She stood on the porch awhile in the shade of the high white columns.

The afternoon had become strangely hot and humid. It was a different sort of weather from any she had known on the island, and she wondered what it might indicate. As she stood there thinking about this, Jethro came along the gravel pathway with a wheelbarrow full of garden weedings which he was taking away for disposal.

He halted and tipped his cap to her. He said, "A hot afternoon, Miss."

"Oddly warm," she agreed. "I've always found the island cool until today."

"A weather breeder," Jethro said, staring bleakly at the almost cloudless sky.

"Weather breeder?"

"That's right, Miss," the handyman said. "You watch and see if we don't have a thunderstorm before midnight. Almost always happens after a day like this."

"There's no sign of a storm now."

"They come up fast," Jethro said.

"I suppose they do."

He picked up the shafts of the wheelbarrow to proceed and vanished around the corner of the house. She valued his Yankee common sense and had come to enjoy her meetings with him.

The oppressive heat made her more conscious of her own threatened plight. She began to think of herself as a hapless victim caught in a spider's web. All the while she was attempting to avenge herself the Copelands were likely weaving their evil plot to eliminate her.

She slowly descended from the porch and strolled across the lawn. This time she avoided the main section of the gardens as she worried that Juliet might be out there with Hudson. She did not want to increase the tensions in that direction. And she could only wonder if Juliet had seen their warm embrace when she spied on them from her window.

Madeline had grown more and more fond of the young

lawyer and she believed that he meant it when he insisted he was going to break his engagement to Juliet. But Juliet was wily and might have something to say about that. The situation was by no means resolved.

If Hudson broke up with the blonde girl, it would be time to take stock of her feelings for him. At the moment she was more concerned with bringing Thomas Copeland to justice. And once she'd accomplished that, things could never be the same between her and Raymond again. The man to whom she'd once been engaged would surely resent her exposing his father as a murderer.

The rest of the family would be indicted as well if she were able to prove that they had tried to murder her and had succeeded in murdering poor Ann Gresham. She no longer was in love with the handsome Raymond; the disenchantment had set in soon after meeting him again on the island. His drinking and his weak character ruined whatever charm he still possessed.

She continued strolling across the broad lawn, avoiding the gardens, and keeping close to the shade of the trees which bordered the lawns. She suddenly found herself only a short distance from the vine-covered summerhouse and was startled to hear voices coming from it. She pressed close to the shelter of the trees so she could not be seen and tried to listen.

The elements were in her favor. Because of the breathless silence in the air accompanying the heat, voices came clearly over a distance. From the summerhouse she heard James Copeland and his father in an agitated exchange.

James was saying, "Too great a risk!"

"We cannot rush," Thomas Copeland said in his calculating fashion.

"I don't like Hudson being here," his older son worried.

"Unfortunate," Thomas coldly agreed.

"And I can't see that it is love for Juliet which has brought him to the island," James went on.

"Probably not," his father said.

"I have the uneasy feeling he is on to something. His getting here for the funeral as he did—"

"You worry too much!" Thomas Copeland snapped.

"And with reason!"

"You lack strength," his father said. "I have not been blessed with children whose character matches my own."

"One minute!" James challenged his father angrily. "I think we have all stood by you beyond the point of reason."

"Why do you say that?"

"It's true. Juliet and I have trusted you implicitly, obeyed you in everything. Gone along with you the full way!"

"Only your duty!" his father snapped.

"And Alice has allowed herself to be a party to it all as well," the young man went on. "Alice is no blood relation. You can't claim that she has any filial debt to you."

"Alice is a fat fool," the older man said in contempt.

"Alice is my wife! I'd ask you to remember that and speak of her with respect."

"Respect," Thomas Copeland said angrily. "After the scene she created, claiming she saw the ghost of Madeline Renais!"

"We did see something. I was with her!" James protested.

"Let's not get into an argument about that nonsense again," his father said. "We have more to fear from the living than from the dead. Like you, I'm strongly suspicious of Hudson Strout."

"What can we do?"

"Nothing for the moment. We may be wrong."

"I think not."

"If he guesses anything he'll give himself away sooner or

later," Thomas Copeland said.

"He and that girl are friends. What do you make of that?"

Thomas said, "He's supposed to have written her aunt's will."

"I can't picture him leaving Boston to go to a country town in Maine for that," James said.

"Nor can I," Thomas agreed. "There is something wrong there."

"I don't trust the girl."

"I've tried to get her off the island," his father said. "I find her difficult to deal with."

"There is always a way," James said with meaning. "You ought to know that better than anyone else."

Madeline was enthralled by the conversation. She felt she was getting an accurate statement of what the two had in their minds. It could aid her in her terrifying situation. But just as James finished hinting that his father make another attempt on her life something startling and unexpected happened.

From a short distance away she heard a joyous bark followed by a whimpering. Her eyes widened with dismay as she saw the great black and white Nero bouncing happily towards her.

Much as she loved the big dog she could think of no moment when he could have been more unwelcome. Certain that his excited barking would attract the attention of the two men in the summerhouse she did the only thing left to her. Blindly she plunged in among the trees. Of course Nero followed her, nuzzling against her and yipping as she tried to calm him.

Bushes scratched against her face and she stumbled over hidden tree roots as she pushed through the woods where no path had been established. The dog enjoyed the lark and kept happily at her side.

She whispered to him reproachfully, "Nero, I thought you were my friend!"

She went on until she thought she'd gone far enough. Then she tried to change her direction so that she could come out of the woods far from the summerhouse. Somehow she lost her way and began to circle blindly in the thick growth. Worst of all the dark, damp woods were infested with blackflies.

She gave Nero an exasperated look and told him, "You've lost me in here, now find the way out!"

The big dog stood straddle-legged watching her, his tail wagging. As soon as she finished speaking, he bounded off and was lost to her. As he vanished she gave a small groan. Now even he had deserted her. She might have expected something like this.

But a few minutes later Nero came bounding back through the thicket noisily. He halted in front of her and barked several times, then he started away again. This time she made an effort to follow him, though her progress through the thick undergrowth was more tortuous than his.

Happily he only went a few yards ahead of her, then paused and turned panting to wait until she caught up. It became a game to him. And she bleakly began to wonder whether he was taking her deeper into the woods or leading her out. The answer came sooner than she'd expected. Suddenly she had a glimpse of the lawn and the old mansion beyond it.

As she emerged in the open she gave a deep sigh of relief. She'd been bitten a few times by blackflies and had a scratch on her cheeks and her dress was soiled at the bottom, otherwise she was all right.

Nero frolicked before her delighted with himself. And then spying a distant cat he raced off, all thought of her gone from his canine mind. She stared after his fast-vanishing black and white body with a rueful smile.

Only then did she notice that Thomas Copeland had been on his way back from the summerhouse and, seeing her, must have become curious. He was alone as he came up to her and with a suspicious look on his face, asked, "What were you doing in the woods?"

She said ruefully, "Nero led me in there. I was foolish enough to follow him. I thought it might be cooler. I didn't count on the blackflies."

"As a country girl you should have," he said. "You were stupid to invade the woods. There are no paths in there plus there's the hazard of a bad swampy area."

"Nero repaired the damage he'd done by leading me out again," she said.

The gaunt man glanced at her soiled skirt and said, "You may consider yourself fortunate. Don't ever go in there again."

"You may be sure I won't," she said.

They began strolling back to the house together. She felt he was still wondering whether she'd been near the summer-house and overheard anything.

He said, "Was that as far on the lawn as you'd gone?"

"Yes," she answered, in an attempt to convince him. "I went into the woods at about the same point I emerged just now."

Thomas Copeland looked grim. "You should really pay more attention to my mother. That is what you are being paid for."

"She wearies of my being around her constantly. It was her wish that I leave for a while."

"I'd go back and check on her now," he said. "This heat must be harder on her than it is on any of us."

"I'll go directly to her," she promised.

And she did as soon as she reached the house. Martha was still sleeping so she crossed to her own room, washed and changed her dress. She also rested for a while before the evening meal.

It grew dark early and the heat remained oppressive. She saw Martha to bed. The old woman kept her word and made no further references to Madeline Renais. Because of the heat, she was in a miserable state and the small effort of being helped into bed left her gasping.

Afterward Madeline walked down the dark hall and out the rear door. She stood outside and saw that the clouds were now gathering to block out the stars. It was a dark, sultry night. The thunderstorm could not be far off.

The door behind her opened and she gave a start. Then she heard Hudson Strout say in a low voice, "My first chance to see you this evening."

"I know," she agreed.

"There's a bad storm in the air."

"Yes," she said. "When it breaks I'm going to try again."

"Become a ghost?"

"Yes, I think it might be the ideal time to confront Thomas Copeland. I know he's guilty."

"I'm on the same floor with him," the young lawyer said. "I'll be on the watch."

"Knowing that will give me courage," she said.

He took her hands in his. "Take care!"

"I will."

"I'm going to worry about you," he promised.

"It will be all right," she told him, though she wasn't by any means sure of it.

"Until later then," he said. And he touched his lips to her forehead and left her.

She remained outside only long enough for him to be on his way. Then she went inside and to her room. When she got there she took a chair and stood on it to retrieve her disguise from the closet shelf where she kept it hidden. Then she sat down before her dresser mirror and went about the task of transforming herself into Madeline Renais once again.

It took the usual patience. And it was almost a half-hour before she donned her black wig and the robe. As she was doing this, she heard the first low rumbles of thunder. Then the storm gradually grew more violent. She crossed to the window and watched the blue lightning forks cut across the black sky. The thunder was like the roar of a great cannon. Soon the drenching rain came and the storm was in full progress.

She knew it was her cue to make a ghostly call on Thomas Copeland. Even though he might be suspicious of her identity, the appearance of Madeline Renais' ghost combined with the eerie background of the storm could have an unexpected effect.

With this in mind she left her room and with pounding heart started down the corridor in the midnight darkness. She came to the stairway and groping for the railing, she slowly made her way upstairs. The thunder came in great crashes which made the old house tremble and the lightning lit up the whole sky.

She reached the door of Thomas Copeland's room and cautiously tried the knob. The door was not locked and gaining courage from this, she turned the handle and slowly opened the door. The lightning came and she had a clear view of the gaunt man, standing fully dressed and gazing out the window at the storm.

Bracing herself she took a few steps further into the dark room. The thunder cannoned and then the vivid blue lightning came again. Thomas Copeland turned from the window and saw her standing there in the eerie light.

"No!" he cried in dismay.

She moved another step towards him, staring at him in ghostly fashion but saying nothing. The lightning came once more to spotlight her.

"Go away!" Thomas Copeland sobbed, holding up his hands in protective fashion. He'd broken within a few seconds.

Elated by her victory, she remained standing where she was waiting for him to cower more before her and admit his guilt. It was then she heard a board creak behind her, she wheeled around just as the lightning flashed. And she saw the black-hooded head of the murderer!

She was at once confused and terrified! She had been so positive that Thomas Copeland was the murderer! Yet now she found herself in the same room with Copeland and the murderer was behind her ready to attack.

It was her turn to stagger back in fear. She vaguely heard Thomas cry out a warning as the room filled with blue light and the horror in the black hood seized her by the throat!

She screamed and tried to free herself. The hooded head was bent close to her and she could hear wild, animal sounds coming from it.

She felt the pressure on her throat and thought she must be going to die at the hands of the phantom after all. Then she was aware of a dark figure looming behind the black hood, something came crashing down on her attacker's head, and in the next moment the clawlike hands released her throat. She stumbled aside, free.

The door from the corridor was thrown open and Hudson Strout and James Copeland appeared in the doorway. James held a lamp high in his hand.

Hudson hurried across the room and took her in his arms. "I didn't want to get here too early," he said. "Are you hurt?"

She shook her head dazedly. "No."

The sight which met her eyes was a strange one. On the floor lay her hooded attacker, the hood still hiding his identity. A few feet distant stood a shattered Thomas Copeland with the barrel end of a rifle in his hands. He had used the butt to fell the would-be murderer.

Hudson Strout turned to the old man. "Who?" he asked, indicating the prostrate figure on the floor.

Thomas seemed in a kind of fog. He didn't make a direct reply to the question. Instead, he murmured, "I hope he's dead! I hope I killed him!"

James came forward with the lamp and set it down on a table near the figure on the floor. In the background the thunder and lightning storm raged on.

James gave her a grim look and knelt down by the motionless figure. He lifted the head and pulled away the black hood to reveal the pale face of Raymond.

"Raymond!" she gasped.

James bent to see if there was any heartbeat. He gave his father a troubled glance. "He's alive," he said. "Better get him out of here before he comes to."

"Yes. He was completely mad when he came in here," the older man agreed.

She stood by in horror as the three men took the limp body from the room. Feeling ill and weak she sank into a nearby chair. She at once remembered that she was disguised to look like her old self and the hastily removed the black wig. It was not a time for charades, she thought dismally as she stared down at it.

Thomas Copeland came back into the room. He stood

there in the glow from the single lamp, looking older than she could ever remember him.

In a taut voice, he said, "Hudson has explained who you are and why you played the ghost of yourself."

"And?"

His lined face was grim. "You were right to think us all guilty, we were in a way. Raymond has been gradually becoming more insane over the past few years and we did our best to conceal this. It began with that illness. The seed of decay was started in his mind. Now it has come to a horrible flowering."

She gave him an accusing look. "You left me to die in the snow!"

"Yes," he sighed. "I did. But it was Raymond who attacked you in one of his violent spells. I thought you were going to die and I had better get you away from the house. In that way he couldn't be blamed. The others helped me get you in the sleigh. We thought you were dead when we left you in that alley."

"And Raymond?"

"When he came to himself he had no memory of attacking you. We rushed him away to Europe and medical treatment there. The treatment did no good and he came back here with Ann Gresham. We knew at once the girl was in terrible danger from him."

"I thought you were the ones," she said in an awed tone. "You were the murderers."

"I'm not surprised," he said.

"Then it was he who started the fire and caused Ann to burn to death?"

"Yes. Again we protected him. I can see I was wrong now. But it is hard to allow your son to be committed to a madhouse."

"You were all shielding him," she said.

"That has been our crime," he said, with a deep sigh. "I shall pay for it through my conscience until my dying day. And I'm willing to take full responsibility before the law. The others mustn't be held to blame. They covered up Raymond's madness at my behest."

That was the revelation. The night and the storm ended and the cool, sunny weather returned to the island. Early in the morning a bound and gagged Raymond was carried struggling into a carriage to be taken across on the ferry to an asylum in Boston. His father and James went with him.

Madeline remained with frail old Martha Copeland until the two men returned. When Thomas was back with his mother once more, Madeline felt she was free to leave. Hudson Strout had stayed on the island with her.

Martha Copeland's mood was sad as she bade Madeline goodbye. "I will miss you," she said. "When we return to Brookline come and visit me."

"I shall," Madeline promised.

Neither Alice nor Juliet appeared to see her off. Hudson had broken his engagement to Juliet, and this, coupled with the shocking events of previous evenings, put her in no frame of mind to say goodbye.

Hudson Strout and Madeline returned to Boston. There Madeline was to rest awhile and then resume her stage career under the guidance of Sam Elder. She appeared only in plays as her singing voice had been permanently damaged. Because her attractiveness had not been marred and she had exceptional talent, she was a great success.

Captain Zachary Miller paused at this point and with a twinkle in his faded, blue eyes, asked Jean, "Do you think that will make a story?"

She looked up from the notes she'd been taking. "It's a wonderful story. Just what I wanted."

"Good!" The old man settled back in his chair with a chuckle.

"But you haven't finished it!" she protested. "What happened to them all?"

"Sorry," the old man said. He stared off into space for a moment. "Hudson Strout and Madeline talked it over and decided to keep it a secret that Raymond had done the murder. Nothing could bring back Ann or change things for Madeline, and Raymond was installed in a lunatic asylum where he died within the year. He was later buried near Ann Gresham in the Dark Harbor family plot."

"What about the others in the family?" she asked.

"Thomas Copeland never got over the tragic business and he died a few months after Raymond," Captain Zachary Miller said. "James and Alice were two of the first to leave here for Florida. He made a fortune in land and died just before the Second World War."

"What about Juliet?" Jean wanted to know.

Captain Zachary Miller smiled at her. "I clean forgot! Well, that young lady had learned her lesson. When she went back to Boston, she called on Madeline and asked her forgiveness and she also made a tearful call on Hudson Strout and told him she didn't blame him for not wanting to marry her."

"That was the right thing for her to do," Jean said, making a note of it.

"Must have been," Captain Zachary chuckled. "To show you how perverse human nature is, he right away decided he loved her after all and did want to marry her. Their grandson comes here every summer in his yacht."

She sat back with a gasp. "Hudson Strout married Juliet?

Then what about Madeline? Don't tell me she married that ugly Sam Elder."

"Nope," the old man said. "Sam was a bachelor by nature and preference. You remember that Dr. Harris who did so much to bring her back to health?"

"Yes," she said breathlessly.

"Well, they met again. He was making a name for himself in private practice by that time and he asked her to marry him and she did. They left Boston after that and lived in New York. They had one daughter. She's an old woman now, about my age. Once in a while she visits the island."

"What a surprise ending," Jean said in amazement. "I can't believe it."

Captain Zachary Miller winked at her. "And the old codgers here in the Pacific Club can't believe how I found myself such an attractive girl."

He saw her to the street and she went back to the hotel full of thoughts of the Copelands and Madeline Renais. There was a phone call waiting for her. It was from Derek Mills at the museum.

"Did you get your story?" he asked.

"Yes, a good one. I'm still in a daze."

"Would you like to have dinner again tonight?" he asked. "I find myself on my own. And I'd like to show you a grave that might interest you along the way."

"I'd enjoy seeing you again," she said. "The same time?"

"Yes. I'll drive by and pick you up."

And he did. She found herself liking the company of the pleasant, brown-haired man. He said, "I suppose now that you have your story you won't stay as long as you planned."

She smiled. "It wouldn't be honest for me to."

"I hope you come back again—on holiday."

"I will," she promised. "Dark Harbor has some sort of

strange spell, it seems. I feel as if I'd been here before and I'm at home."

"I've heard others say that," Derek Mills agreed. He headed the car along a side road and came to a halt at the entrance to an old cemetery. With a smile, he told her, "The Captain asked me to bring you here to prove he didn't make the story up."

"There's no need," she protested but she did get out of the car and follow him into the ancient and neglected old cemetery.

At her side, Derek pointed out, "You can see the bayberry bushes and weeds have taken over. And the tombstones are falling down. But the Old North Cemetery was the main burial place once. And it is here the Copelands had their family lot."

They reached a place where two small gray stones leaned at drunken angles. Derek knelt by them and pulled aside some weeds. "Most of the inscriptions are worn away," he said. "But you can still read the names."

Jean bent close and saw faintly on one stone in fancy script, the name "Ann Gresham." The other inscription read "Raymond Copeland", and beneath that, "Repent my sins." Her eyes unexpectedly moistened. It all seemed so real to her and yet it had happened so long ago. She said, "How soon people forget!"

Derek nodded. And then they turned and made their way out of the old cemetery, arm in arm.